The Injustice

Contents

Chapter 1

Clive felt like a lump of dough on a conveyor belt, slowly making its way through the scorching oven on its journey to being bread. The holiday traffic was a nightmare in the heat and the air blurred and steamed as it baked off the surface of the road.

Clive was sweating and the edge of his short brown hair was damp where it met his brow. He switched on the air con for another burst of cold air to fill the car. He didn't like to leave it on too long as he'd heard that it lowers fuel economy.

He looked over at his wife, Lila, sat in the passenger seat. She didn't seem bothered by the heat one bit. The small amount of makeup that she wore was still perfect. Her brown hair, with the blue streak dyed into the fringe, sat softly on her shoulders, dry as a bone. She was just so much cooler than he was, in attitude and temperature, and looks wise was in a league way above Clive's. He often wondered what she was doing with a guy like him, but tried not to think too much about it as it made him nervous.

He felt really lucky to have met a woman like Lila, but why had she chosen this day of all days to go to the zoo?

Cars were sat end to end on the road, rolling slowly forward inches at a time. The kids in the car in front were acting up, jumping around, fighting and Clive could see the father turning round to chastise them every few minutes, so distracted by asserting his authority that he wasn't keeping up with the flow of traffic and was making progress even slower. *Why do people put themselves through this every school holiday?* Clive thought to himself.

In hindsight Clive knew he should've booked a day off work and taken Lila to the zoo when it was quiet but she wouldn't have been happy with that. She liked to have days out at times when other people were having days out. She liked to watch the families picnicking on the grass, see the kids giggle as their parents pushed them on the swings and coo at the babies all snuggled up in their prams, fantasising about herself being in the role of the mother.

Clive knew it was his fault, although the doctor's hadn't said this directly. He knew it was something wrong with him. The doctors keep telling them that there is nothing wrong, that nature will take its course, and to be patient because they were still young, but he knew he was defective.

He had never been the picture of good health and, although he didn't eat much, what he ate was full of carbohydrates and fat. Add this to the lack of any real exercise and the disproportionate largeness of his belly compared to his arms and legs wasn't so hard to explain. No wonder he struggled to provide his wife with a child.

"Clive. You're driving like an old lady stop crawling and overtake this guy," said Lila in her usual direct manner. She rarely spoke to Clive without calling him some sort of name. Usually it rolled of his back, sometimes it annoyed him but mostly he'd gotten used to it and didn't even notice.

"That's not fair. This guy wants to get where he's going just as much as we do," he answered in his usual fair approach to everything.

"Pussy!" she called him. That one annoyed him.

She folded her slender frame up to rest her feet on the shiny black plastic of the dash.

Clive looked at her then looked at her feet. She got the message and took them down.

"You might think it's soft but if it was us in that car then you'd be annoyed if someone overtook us. If we all had a bit more patience with each other this city would be a much better place."

"Whatever Grandma," she replied back.

Clive let out a heavy breath of air through his nose.

Lila's emerald green eyes light up and her lips puckered, suppressing her smile of enjoyment in winding up her husband. She tucked her hair behind her ears, turned up the song by the latest teenage mega pop star and sang along to the words of the chorus. Her voice didn't match the delicate beauty of her looks as it cracked and wavered over the long notes but this didn't bother her. She was enjoying herself and as long as Lila was happy she didn't really care what anyone else thought or did.

Clive thumbed the control on his steering wheel to turn the music back down.

"Hey!" she said slapping him on the arm. "I was listening to that."

"You can still hear it and I need to concentrate."

"Concentrate on what? We're crawling along in traffic," she said as she folded her arms and flung herself back hard against the seat.

A black Audi sped past them and swerved in front of Clive. Clive slammed on the brakes to avoid hitting the back of it.

Clive gestured with the open palms of his hands at the Audi. "See what I mean?" he asked looking at Lila. Clive pressed his horn. "Asshole," he said loudly, exaggerating his lips, safe inside his car.

The brake lights of the Audi lit up and it stopped. An overweight guy with a crew cut and a checked shirt got out and walked towards Clive's car with his hands clenched into fists. The man was massive and as he got nearer he started to dwarf Clive's little Hyundai hatchback. Clive regretted calling the man a name and looked over his shoulder hoping for a police car to appear.

"What did you call me?" the man growled at Clive's window.

Clive wound it down an inch so he could talk back. "I just don't think you should be cutting people up like that. You're no more important than anyone else," he said keeping his eyes looking forward, afraid to make eye contact.

The man turned his head to the side and smiled through a clenched jaw. "You know what? Get out, wise guy and we'll see who's important," he said as he grabbed the door handle to open the door. The handle pulled loosely in his hand but the door didn't open.

Clive always locked the doors on a car journey in case of carjackers or bag snatchers but now he'd add road rage to the list of reasons to do it on future trips.

"Go away fatty," shouted Lila as she leaned across Clive to shout through the open window.

"Shh," hushed Clive pushing her back to her own side of the car. "Look, there's no need to get violent. No one's injured and there's no damage. Let's just get back in our cars and go on our way."

"Come on," shouted the guy banging on the roof of Clive's car. "Let's sort this out man to man."

"Get ready to dial the police," Clive said to Lila.

The guy banged on Clive's window again rocking the car with the force of his blow. "Come on tough guy, you called me an asshole. Come and say it to my face."

"I'm calling the police," warned Clive.

The guy put his arms on his waist and shook his head in disappointment. "Pussy," he spat. He grabbed hold of Clive's wing mirror and ripped it from the car then let it drop so it dangled on the wires that controlled its electric motor. Happy with his work the man walked back to his car.

"Quick get your camera so I can take a picture of his license plate," said Clive without taking his eyes off the man. Lila handed him her camera and he held it up just above the dashboard, so the man didn't see it, and snapped a picture. "That might come in handy if there's a crime reported involving a black Audi. We can hand it in to the police. He looked like a criminal."

"Oh Clive Silver, you're so brave. My hero," said Lila in a high pitched voice before giggling at herself as she mocked her husband.

Clive ignored her, it was always best to ignore her in these situations. He set back off into the traffic but his leg was trembling and he jerked forward, kangarooing the first few metres. Lila giggled louder.

"It's not funny you know. That's gonna cost money to fix and that guy could've had a knife or gun or anything. We could have been seriously hurt there and what if we had kids with us." He stopped there realising he'd accidently brought up the one subject they didn't talk about. Now neither of them knew what to say next and an awkward silence filled the car. Suddenly a little run in with an angry motorist didn't seem so important in the bigger picture.

"You're right. There's no point getting into a fight you can't win just to save face. You did the right thing," Lila replied breaking the silence. "What'ya gonna do about the damage?"

"I'll have a look at it when we get to the zoo. Hopefully it'll just clip back on otherwise I'm sending that picture to the insurance company and telling them to contact his insurers for the cost of repairs."

"That's a good idea," she agreed. "Let's forget about this and get to the zoo?"

Clive smiled at his wife. "OK."

Barely ten minutes had passed when another car sped past and cut in front of them. This time it was a police car and the lights were flashing. The police car slowed down and the officer inside pointed to the edge of the road. Clive pulled over.

"They probably want to ask me about the Audi driver," said Clive as he opened his door and got out.

"Stay in the car please Sir," said a tall, slim, bald officer wearing mirrored shades.

Clive dropped back into his seat and lowered his window. The officer approached and leaned inside the car. His bald head shining so close to Clive's face that he could see his own reflection. The officer pulled the key from the ignition, looked at Lila and smiled.

"You know it's a legal requirement to have working wing mirrors don't you?" he asked Clive sternly.

"Yes officer, but you see..."

The officer raised his index finger and Clive stopped talking. "You are aware that you're wing mirror is broken aren't you?"

"Yes officer."

The officer wrote something down in the little notebook he'd taken out of his pocket.

"Are you writing me a ticket?" Clive asked the officer in shock

"Yes sir," said the officer without looking up from his writing.

"That's absolutely ridiculous," said Clive.

The officer looked over his shades directly at Clive. His eyebrows lowered slightly. "Excuse me, sir?"

"You haven't even asked me why my wing mirror is broken."

"By law you must have functioning wing mirrors on your vehicle and you, by your own admission, are aware that yours are broken. This requires me to give you a ticket which is a fixed penalty. If you so wish to appeal the ticket then you can do so via the number on the back at which point your case may be heard in a court and you will have every opportunity to put forward your story then."

"If you just let me show you one thing," said Clive as he leant over to retrieve the camera from the glove compartment.

The officer drew his weapon and aimed it at Clive. "Stop what you're doing and slowly step out of the vehicle," he said speaking loudly and clearly. By now the other officer had noticed his partners drawn weapon and got out of the police car. He aimed his gun at Clive from behind the shield of the police car door.

"Oh wait. No. I was just getting my camera," stuttered Clive.

The officer cocked his gun. "Get out of the vehicle. Hands where I can see 'em."

Clive opened his door and raised his hands in the air.

"Turn around," commanded the officer.

Clive slowly turned around, his hands still pointing to the sky. The officer slammed him face first into the hood then twisted his arms behind his back and tightened cuffs round his wrists. Clive was dragged back to the police car and thrown in the back, the door slammed shut behind him. The plastic covered seats felt hot against Clive's skin where they'd been baking in the sun. The car stank of bleach failing to mask the smell of urine and vomit from the countless dirty drunks that, over the years, had occupied the same space that Clive was now sat in. Clive perched as far on the edge of the seat as he could manage trying to make the least contact between him and the seat.

The other officer, a short guy with ginger hair and a flushed red complexion got back in the car. He looked at Clive in the rear view mirror then picked his phone off the dash and started texting. Clive sighed, it was just his luck. He should've listened to Lila and overtook that car and then they might have been at the zoo right now.

Through the windshield Clive could see that Lila was being approached by the bald officer. He was smiling at her as she got out of the car unchallenged. Clive knew the type of guy the officer was, one rule for a pretty lady and a different rule for everyone else. Creep.

Lila's lips moved as she explained something to the officer but Clive couldn't make out the words. She reached back into the car, pulled out the camera and showed it to the officer. He leaned in to her pressing their bodies together side by side as they both looked at the picture on the screen of the camera. They both laughed and he said something into his radio as he walked back to the car where Clive was sat waiting.

"We're going to have to deal with this down the station," said the bald officer as he slid back in to the driver's seat of the police car.

"What about my wife?" asked Clive.

"I've radioed in for another car to pick her up and take her to the zoo," he said.

"And my car?"

"It'll be impounded and won't be released until it's in a roadworthy condition."

"But how am I supposed to get it in a roadworthy condition if it's in the impound?"

"Not my problem I'm afraid. You'll have to speak to the guy at the impound."

Clive closed his eyes and thought about his bad day. He thought about the Audi driver and how he was probably at the zoo right now enjoying a day out with his wife and kids whilst Clive, who had done nothing wrong, was in a police car being charged for a nonsense crime he didn't commit. Talk about injustice.

The second police car arrived and Lila got into it, assisted by the sleazy bald officer smiling and holding her arm as he did so.

Clive was angry. He had always thought the police would have his back, look after him, protect him but now they were treating him like a common criminal and flirting with his wife at the same time.

He was also afraid. He had never been in a police station before and worried about being thrown in a cell with some violent criminal.

Chapter 2

Clive squeezed his car in between a rusty old wreck and a dumpster at the back of the zoo parking lot, the last empty space he could find. He walked for what seemed miles through the rows and rows of cars until he got to the entrance and there, he saw a van parked across 2 spaces.

"Selfish," whispered Clive to himself.

He took the name of the company scrawled on the side, Ekron Water Company, and promised himself he'd report it to them when he got home. Clive hated the Ekron Water Company. Shoreline City was built between a vast mountain range and the coast. The water from the mountains ran underground and into the ocean. The Ekron Water Company mined the water from the ground and charged the citizens a hefty price for it, knowing that it was their only choice.

Clive always thought it was a stupid place to build a city anyway. It was miles away from any other decent sized settlement and there was no airport, so to get out you had to either drive the miles up and over the mountain range or take a boat and go slowly along the coast by water.

"One adult please," he said to the lady at the turnstile. She gave him a suspicious look wondering why a single adult male would be going to the zoo during the school holidays. "My wife's already inside," he said to answer her unspoken question.

He paid the lady and stepped through into the bustling zoo full of kids with stuffed animals and ice-creams. He tilted his head back and let the sun warm his face. He'd got here at last and felt the stress drain out of him.

In a way it had kind of been his lucky day. If it wasn't for that urgent call out the officers got he would have been in a police station right now, no doubt filling out pointless forms and waiting it out in a cell whilst some inept glorified clerk in a uniform stamped them and released him.

His phone vibrated in his pocket and a picture of Lila pulling a goofy face flashed on the screen.

"Hi honey," he answered. "I've just got in now. I'm at the turnstile. Where are you?"

"I'm by the lions. Hurry up there's a sea lion show on soon and I don't want to miss it," she replied.

"Right. See you in a minute."

He looked at the map of the zoo that the lady at the turnstile gave him. On the map were cutesy little drawings of the animals at the zoo and none of them were particularly clear. He found the lions and guessed they could be on one of two paths so after twirling the map upside down so that it was positioned relative to the direction he was facing, he set off.

The throng of people walking through the zoo were all strolling slowly as they enjoyed their day out in the sun. Clive's pace was much faster as he rushed to Lila and he found himself becoming more and more agitated. A woman pushing an empty twin buggy, her two toddlers on reins walking beside her, was talking up the whole path in front of Clive. He took a deep breath and tried to remember he was supposed to be relaxing. One of the toddlers fell and the woman rushed over to help it up and Clive took his opportunity to go past them through the empty gap she left.

He reached a crossroads and stopped to check the map.

"Excuse me. You couldn't tell me how to get to the sea lions could ya?" asked a fat lump of a man in brightly coloured red shorts with yellow flowers, a blue t-shirt that struggled to cover his belly and a baseball cap with sunglasses combo. Clive wondered why he needed both sets of sun protection unless he was a vampire scared of the daylight. Then he realised that vampires only live off of blood, which this guy clearly didn't.

"Erm," said Clive fumbling with his map. "Well I guess we're here, and the sea lions are there, so it's a left down that path over there."

The man leaned against Clive, his warm, damp, squishy arm flab touching Clive as he peered at the map.

"Those are manatee's buddy. I said sea lions," said the man jabbing his sausage finger at the map.

"No I think they're sea lions. It's just a bad drawing."

"Don't worry," said the chubster as he waddled away with the rest of his XXXL family in tow. *His constant craving for food obviously affected his ability to concentrate on a map*, thought Clive.

Clive looked at the map again and checked his bearing before setting off to find Lila.

Eventually he got to the lions and looked around for the slim figure of his wife, but apart from a kissing couple and their young boy, who had pressed his face against the fence and was screaming roaring noises at the lions, there was no one here. He got out his phone.

"Where are you?" he asked.

"Oh I got bored of the lions so I'm by the giraffes now," she answered.

"Right wait there."

He didn't need to check the map this time. He could see the long necks of the giraffes extending out in the distance.

"Where have you been?" asked Lila as he approached.

"Never mind, come on let's get to this show. I need a sit down."

"Right then. This way," pointed Lila.

Clive looked at his map again. "I'm pretty sure it's this way," he said showing her the map.

"Well I think this way is better but let's go with your idea."

Clive hoped he was right. She'd given up on her idea too easily and he knew it would be thrown back at him if he was wrong and they missed the show.

They reached the entrance to the sea lion show and stood in the long queue to get inside. The queue snaked in a zigzag alongside a large round patch of fenced off open grass. Clive bent his knees and angled his body to try and catch a glimpse of what was inside the enclosure but saw nothing and the little door that separated the sleeping enclosures was closed.

Clive was growing anxious. The show started soon and the line wasn't even moving. He checked his watch again. Two minutes to show time.

"Good idea Clive. This queue is massive," said Lila sarcastically. "If we went my way we'd be over that side now in that much smaller queue," she continued pointing at the other side of the empty enclosure. "Plus we'll probably end up sat behind that guy." Lila moved her finger to point at the fat family that Clive had directed earlier.

"Oh damn," said Clive instantly losing his cool. "Right let's do it your way then," he said.

"Don't get mad at me Clive Silver," said Lila. "It's not my fault you don't listen. Anyway we'll never make it round the paths in time for the start of the show.

Clive looked around to see if any zoo staff were around and said "Come on. We can go through here."

"No way that's an animal enclosure," said Lila.

"I've checked. It's empty. I think it's closed for maintenance or something."

"Alright if you think it's safe," said Lila. Clive could hear the reluctance in her voice.

Clive jumped down into the shallow enclosure and helped Lila down. It was a bit of a drop but nothing he couldn't manage. Whatever they usually kept in here obviously wasn't a great jumper.

Behind them they heard gasps from the people stood in the queue but Clive told himself to ignore them. *Why should he care what they think?*, he told himself. Even though he did care and felt embarrassed that people might think bad of him but he'd had enough of sticking to the rules and always losing out. For once he was going to break them and gain something. He deserved that especially after the day he'd had.

Halfway across the enclosure he heard a sound like a broken, high pitched chatter. He stopped in his tracks. Had he made a mistake? Was the enclosure empty? He couldn't remember if he'd made absolutely sure.

Something jumped across their path and ran into the corner of the enclosure, it was a hyena.

Lila screamed, which drew the instant attention of everyone stood around the enclosure who wasn't already watching them.

The hyena jumped on its back legs and chattered in excitement before running around the enclosure. It was testing them unsure how dangerous these intruders were in its enclosure.

Clive panicked and ran back for the wall where they had dropped into the enclosure but he came straight back realising he'd left Lila. He grabbed her arm to lead her away but her legs had frozen in fear and he pulled her over.

Clive put his hands under her arms and tried to pull her back up on her feet.

The hyena ran over again and snapped its massive black jaws at them making a sound like the soles of two shoes being slapped together before retreating back into the corner. With each run it made at them it was getting closer and Clive knew the next one could be a bite.

Clive was terrified and he remembered a documentary he saw once saying that hyenas jaws are some of the most powerful in the animal kingdom. He imagined his head, or even worse Lila's, being crushed between the animal's teeth.

A handful of zoo keepers had reached the enclosure and were leaning over the edge banging their hands on the walls to scare the hyena away from them but instead it was just exciting the animal, whipping it up into a frenzy.

Clive tried to pull Lila up again but she was a dead weight, leaden in his hands. He looked at the hyena and let go of Lila as he fought with his instincts to run away.

Another man had entered the enclosure. He was wearing the green combat trousers and matching green top of the keeper's uniform and completed the look with his pierced eyebrow and his save the earth Greenpeace long scruffy hair tied back in a ponytail. He was thrusting a broom out in front of him and shouting random noises to push the hyena back as he made his way towards Clive and Lila.

"Here take this," he said to Clive handing him the broom. "Wave it around in front of him and make loud noises. It'll scare him off." The keeper grabbed Lila and threw her over his shoulder. "Come on follow me," he beckoned to Clive.

Clive waved the broom side to side making large swipes. He tried shouting but his voice broke and his throat ached whenever he made a noise.

The keeper made his way slowly to the edge of the enclosure and the hoisted Lila up to another keeper who pulled her to safety. He then pulled himself up and turned to reach his arm out to Clive.

Clive was slowly walking backwards towards the keeper's outstretched arm and the hyena was following him, matching him step for step. Clive's back hit the edge of the enclosure and stopped him but the hyena kept making slow steps towards him. The gap between them decreasing slowly.

"Grab my hand," shouted the keeper.

Clive took a quick glance at the keeper whose torso was hanging down from the railing with his arm outstretched towards Clive.

Clive looked back at the hyena and looked in its black eyes. He felt like it knew it had separated the weak one from the herd. He imagined the animal pouncing forward and ripping at his windpipe.

"Come on man. Grab my hand," shouted the keeper again.

Clive turned quickly and grabbed the keepers arm, locking their wrists together but Clive was panicking and instead of jumping he just lifted his feet off the ground and swung from the keepers arm.

The keeper tried to pull Clive to safety but he just wasn't strong enough to lift all that weight from that angle.

Clive flailed his legs around trying to get a purchase on the edge of the enclosure so he could push himself up to safety. He wished he made more effort to go to the gym, to lift weights, to play a sport anything that would have meant his arms were strong enough to pull his body weight up right now.

He sensed the air get thicker, the tensions rise and amongst all the noise he heard a woman let out a scream. It wasn't that other women weren't screaming but the scream of this particular woman was different. There was something about it that Clive's mind had singled it out from the rest of the noise. Then he realised what was special about it, he'd heard Lila make a similar one when the monster jumped out in whatever horror film they were watching and attacked the helpless victim.

The hyena bit his leg. At first it was a hot pain like someone had sandwiched his leg between two hot irons. Then it subdued, the pain became more acute and he could feel each of the hyena's teeth ripping into his skin. The shock made him let go of the keepers and he fell to the floor of the enclosure. He passed out before he hit the ground.

Chapter 3

"Clive... Clive... Can you hear me Clive?" said the paramedic crouched over Clive's motionless body. The voice distorted inside Clive's head like the two of them were underwater. "You've lost a lot of blood and we're going to take you to the hospital do you understand?" she said.

A crowd have formed a wide circle around him giving the paramedics enough room to work but staying close enough to see the detail. His arms, legs and body were covered in blood stained bandages like a half dressed Egyptian mummy. A few onlookers took pictures illuminating the scene like a Hollywood red carpet.

Lila stood sobbing, looking on as the scene unfolded before her hoping he'd be ok. Clive's head wallowed side to side as he slid back into consciousness. He blinked his eyes open and shut.

The paramedic reached into her case and ripped open the seal on a new syringe. She stabbed it into a small vial and drew back the plunger. "This is going to ease the pain. Ok Clive?" she said as she sunk the needle into his arm and emptied the contents into his veins. Clive felt the cold liquid running through his arm.

A pair of policemen had arrived and one of them started taping off the scene whilst the other chatted to the paramedic and Lila scribbling down details as they talked.

Another zookeeper approached Clive, a giant man with dark skin and muscles bulging through his green shirt. He crouched over Clive and looked into his eyes.

"Ah I see you are still alive," he said with a thick Nigerian accent. "Perhaps this may help your recovery." He pulled out a syringe, jabbed it into Clive's neck before slamming down the plunger and disappearing faster than he appeared.

Clive's vision turned red, then black and he was gone again, unconscious.

Chapter 4

The nurse ticked the final box on her list, looked up at Clive and shook her head in disbelief. She replaced the clipboard back on the end of the bed and left him alone with Lila.

"The doctors tell me that they've never seen anyone recover so fast in their life. The stitches are already out and the bruising is almost gone. They say you're a medical marvel. I told them I always knew you were a bit of a freak," said Lila with a smile.

"Very funny. Did they say when I can leave?" asked Clive.

"Not for a few more days. They want to keep you under observation," answered Lila.

"But I'm ok. They're probably just after more money from the insurance company, Doctor's on the take, you read about it all the time."

"They expected you to be in a coma for weeks, your heart stopped for so long there was a high risk of brain damage so you can understand their caution. Although there isn't much up there to damage if you ask me."

"I'm intelligent. In fact I'd say my brain was probably my best feature," protested Clive.

"Of course you're intelligent. Taking a shortcut through the hyena enclosure and dragging your poor wife along with you. That's an intelligent thing to do."

"I've said I'm sorry. The enclosure looked empty. It didn't even look like an enclosure the sides weren't very high. They should have warning signs on that thing. I should sue them."

"They probably thought there was no point. There's no way anyone stupid enough to go into an enclosure at the zoo is going to be able to read." Lila looked at him waiting for a reaction but Clive was feeling too guilty and let her have that one. "Anyway I'm not having you risk Brian's job. That man risked his life to save us and if it wasn't for him we would both be dead."

The sound of that man's name sparked resentment in Clive. "Did you notice that the hyena seemed to stay away from him? I bet super Brian beats that poor hyena with that brush when nobody's looking," he said snipingly.

"How dare you say that about him after what he did for you? Did you realise that he saved your wife's life whilst you stood there and peed your pants like a little girl. When have you done anything brave, eh?"

Clive closed his eyes and took a deep breath to calm down. He knew he should be grateful to the guy but couldn't help feeling jealous that his wife was idolising another man. "Ok so the guy saved you and I owe him a massive debt of gratitude but he knows about these animals. He probably knew how it would react. If I'd had the same training I bet I could've handled it just as well as he did."

"No Clive you are a wimp, a coward, a yellow belly. If bravery involved angry letter writing you'd be a hero. If courage was defined as complaining you'd win a medal of honour. Unfortunately for you it's neither of those things and, even with all the training in the world, when push comes to shove, you run."

"Yeah well Brian has hair like a girl," responded Clive childishly.

"Well I like his hair and if I don't hurry I'm going to miss my dinner with him," said Lila picking up her bag and swinging it over her shoulder.

"He's taking you to dinner?"

"No I'm taking him. To say thank you for saving me and we may even go out for drinks after although he did say he might not be able to stay out long because he's looking after an orphaned koala bear at his house and it needs feeding round the clock. Bye Clive."

Lila spun on her heel and walked off quickly making sure she left before Clive could respond and she had the last word.

"Baby koala really? What a sleaze ball. I bet he tells that to all the chicks," muttered Clive to himself.

The hours ticked by and Clive thought about nothing but his wife out on a date with that long haired, baby koala loving, hyena beating scoundrel. No wait it wasn't a date it was just dinner and Clive told himself he could trust Lila but if he was honest he'd always known he wasn't good enough for Lila. Perhaps she's starting to realise that and is going after someone more exciting. He even has a baby already, albeit a baby koala but it's still better than Clive could provide.

It was just over a week ago today that they'd been talking about children when they decided to go to the zoo to take their mind off of the stress of 5 months' worth of unsuccessful trying. A happy family in the planning. Now, in his mind at least, she'd left him for Brian. How could it fall apart so quickly?

He felt himself getting angry and then feeling stupid because nothing had actually happened yet. He was getting angry over his imagination.

It was this place. The lack of entertainment was making his mind wander into areas he didn't want it to go. He texted Lila to apologise for being mean about Brian and then concentrated on putting it out of his mind. At first he did sums in his head but this wasn't going to keep him going for long so he looked around at the other patients with visitors and tried to listen in on their conversations like a kind of live action floor show.

In the bed over by the door was a man who'd been in a car accident that had crushed his lower legs. He occasionally wheeled round the ward on the wheelchair they'd given him whistling away like the happiest man in the world. His conversation with his visitor was about how lucky he'd been not to die in the crash. *Stupid idiot,* thought Clive. *He should feel unlucky for being in the accident in the first place. Right now he could be relaxing at home sat in his favourite armchair instead of a wheelchair.*

The man by the nurse's station was much grimmer. He moaned and groaned at the pain until someone came and topped up his meds then he was out like a light for a few hours. He had gotten his arm trapped in some sort of digger. *I thought manual labourers were supposed to be tough.* No one ever visits him but today he had a visitor. Clive couldn't see the visitor because the curtain was pulled round blocking his view but from his shadow he looked like a big guy, probably the digger driver that crushed his arm feeling guilty and paying him a visit. It's a shame he's just had a top up of meds so he's knocked out cold, probably would've been grateful of someone to talk to.

And then there's Frank in the bed next to Clive's. He had lots of visitors and well-wishers. This guy was sombre and soaked up the sympathy when people were here but when they left he'd be up and about telling Clive which of his attractive lady visitors he'd slept with and which ones he intended to. Clive doubted his stories but he let him tell them because it beat staring at that crooked ceiling tile above Clive's bed which was his only other option for entertainment outside of visiting hours. The person who visited Frank most of all was his lawyer. Frank had been injured by a wardrobe collapsing on to him when he was looking round one of these giant home furnishing stores. His injuries weren't really that bad but Frank had sniffed the chance to make money and was chasing that scent all the way to the bank. Between him and his lawyer they'd spend hours documenting his pain and suffering making sure the wording of his claim was exactly right like it would form part of the next bible.

Frank's lawyer was here again and Clive rolled to face them so he could listen in on their conversation.

"Tell me about the neck. It looks sore. Still I bet there's no movement there at all is there?" asked his lawyer.

Frank stiffly turned his neck slightly to the right before wincing with pain. "No man it's completely shot."

"Would you say the pain was unbearable?"

"Yeah, unbearable or maybe excruciating. No, unbearable. That's the one. It's unbearable man I can't stand it much longer. It's driving me crazy."

"It can be unbearable and excruciating at the same time," his lawyer prompted him.

"Yeah. Ok then. Both."

"You must be suffering emotional effects as well. It must be hard for you. I bet you're having nightmares aren't you?"

"Oh hell yeah, freaky ones about wardrobes eating me up and stuff. I wake up in a hot sweat," said Frank.

"Sounds horrific. So you're not able to get much sleep then?"

"Nope. Before the accident I'd be out like a light as soon as my head hit the pillow and I'd sleep through solid like a baby too. Couldn't get a chainsaw or a jumbo jet to wake me up I slept that deeply. Now it takes me ages to get to sleep and then I dream I'm a snack at a dinner party for furniture and I wake up screaming, too scared to go back to sleep."

Clive couldn't remember ever hearing Frank scream in the night. Perhaps he dreamed about waking up and screaming and it was all one multi layered mega dream or more likely it was just crap.

"Clive," whispered a voice in a deep Nigerian accent.

Clive sat up quickly and checked the visitor's chair next to his bed but it was empty. He looked at Frank and his lawyer but they hadn't looked in his direction.

"Clive," said the whisper again.

"Can I help you?" said Clive still trying to work out where the whisper was coming from. Frank and his lawyer turned and looked at Clive strangely trying to work out who he was talking to.

"You alright there buddy?" asked Frank.

"Yeah I'm fine," said Clive settling back down into his bed.

"No one else can hear me Clive. It looks as though you're talking to yourself," whispered the voice inside his head.

Clive sat back up in his bed, rubbed his face and took a sip of water.

"Don't be alarmed Clive," said the voice.

Clive looked around the hospital in panic hoping to see an actual person trying to talk to him. Frank and his lawyer were still deliberating over which part of his body hurt most. The guy in the wheelchair was showing his sister how he could tie his own shoelaces and the guy next to the nurses' station was still out cold from his meds, the shadow of his visitor sat motionless.

Clive concentrated his mind and tried to talk back. *Who are you?* he asked. There was no response.

"Clive," said the voice again.

By now Clive had begun to sweat and was panicking. He valued his mind above all other things. He'd rather had lost a leg to the hyena than go bonkers afterwards.

"CLIVE!" screamed the voice in his head.

No, thought Clive. He concentrated on other things. He thought about his wife, his house, the trip to the zoo, anything.

"Listen to me," said the voice.

Clive started singing a song in his head. *I'm not listening, I can't hear you, I'm not going mad.* His head nodded along to the beat. He made his body move, his mind think and breathed rhythmically. He was trying his best to block the madness.

His concentration was broken by the clatter of a chair falling over and skidding along the hospital floor. The friend of the comatose whinger next to the nurses' station had stood up suddenly and was glaring at Clive with a face of fury. Clive was right he was a big man with huge square shoulders pulling his shirt tight round his muscles. His jet black pupils burned into Clive and Clive thought he recognised him. He'd seen him somewhere before but he couldn't work out where. His mind was unable to look into the past for fear of what was stood before him in the present.

Clive was scared. He was hooked up to an intravenous drip and blood pressure monitor and he felt very vulnerable in front of this giant, angry man.

The man grunted and stormed off the ward leaving behind a very relieved Clive. He looked around and everyone else was carrying on as normal. Had he imagined that?

Chapter 5

Clive had been sent home from hospital completely healed. He'd gained some cool scars where his wounds had healed over. *Chicks dig a guy with scars,* he told himself. But there was more than just resealed skin that had happened to Clive. His body had begun to change as well. His upper arms had grown a curve on his bicep where before it was flat as an open bottle of month old soda. His chest had begun to broaden and the outlines of pecs were visible. He was in the greatest shape of his life and Lila couldn't resist a quick squeeze of his firm buttocks or to run her fingers over his washboard stomach every time she got near him.

The doctor had given him 6 weeks off work to recover so Clive was clearing out the garage. It's something that had been nagging at him but he'd never gotten round to before. He needed to make room for the buggies and crib's and other baby paraphernalia that was being donated to them by Lila's sister.

Ever since her sister had given birth Lila had fawned over the baby. Clive knew the expectations would be on him to deliver the next addition to the extended family. He worried that, at 23 years old, people would say they were too young to have a baby but he justified it to himself. They had good jobs, a house, were married and neither of them were the type to be going out all hours drinking and partying. Not that they ever needed these excuses with Lila's family. They'd just presumed they would start trying and offloaded every item of equipment and clothing as soon as it was no longer needed.

The blame for the baby not already being on the way was clearly pointed at Clive. After all, Lila's family were proven breeders with both her older sisters and her brother already having kids. Every time they came to visit Clive could feel the blame they put on him for not producing a child already.

He started pulling the larger items out of the way like the lawnmower, the barbeque and a wheelbarrow to clear some space so he could see what he could throw away. He took some old boxes off of the shelf and started sorting through them stopping every now and then when he found something interesting he'd forgotten about, like his original Xbox with controllers and a handful of games. Although he knew he'd never play on it again he wasn't getting rid of it. Some of his fondest memories from his childhood were sat at this console. In fact he'd spent a lot of time with Lila playing this console back when they were just friends in high school.

He was struggling to find stuff he could clear out. Most things he found might be useful at some point in the future. It would be pointless throwing them out and then having to buy a new one when it was needed. So far he'd taken out an old computer monitor, a pair of Lila's old rollerblades and some old tins of paint. Not exactly a major transformation.

He took a step back to view his work and tripped over a box of Christmas decorations. He fell on to the sharp metal shelving that lined one wall of the garage and felt the edge graze down his left arm scratching away the skin. When he landed his right hand instinctively went to cover the graze. He got to his knees again and moved his right hand to see blood. *Damn*, he thought to himself for being so clumsy and went inside to wash off the blood.

He ran the graze under the water expecting to feel a sting as the cold water entered the wound but there was nothing. He washed away the blood to see only perfect unbroken skin. He checked his right hand to see if the cut was there but that was fine as well. He twisted his arm checking underneath, puzzled at where the blood had come from. He definitely remembered the sharp feeling of the graze as he fell.

Back out in the garage he checked around to see if it was old paint or something else that he'd fallen in, but there was nothing.

He grabbed a screw from the shelf and slowly scratched it across his arm drawing a white line where it tore the top layer of the skin. The white line vanished, undoing itself as though time was being rewound, leaving behind perfect smooth skin. He did it again, this time gouging deeper into the skin, feeling the sting as the white line grew with dots of red as it drew blood. Again the white line unmarked itself as though it was closing a zip that Clive had just opened. He licked his finger and wiped away the blood unable to find the mark where he had been cut.

He put the screw back and picked up a hacksaw. This was stupid he was cutting himself on purpose but he had to know what would happen. He rested the blade on his arm, drew a deep breath and dragged it quickly over his skin. The blade cut deep and blood seeped from the gash. Clive regretted his action instantly as the blood ran down his arm and dripped to the floor. He dropped the saw and pressed his free hand on the wound and ran inside again to wash it, being careful not to spill any blood on the carpet as he went.

When the water washed away the blood, the cut was closed but his arm was not completely unmarked. A faint scar was left where the hacksaw had cut.

Clive's stomach bubbled like a witch's cauldron and he lurched forward over the sink, vomiting bile down the plughole. He splashed his face with water and took a sip of mouthwash to swill away the taste of sick. Was this really happening? He had thought he was hearing voices in the hospital and worried he was losing his mind. Was this another step in his loss of sanity?

One last test, he told himself as he grabbed his razor from the cabinet. He took the head off of the handle and held the blade in his hand against his arm. He took a deep breath and closed his eyes psyching himself up to intentionally cut himself.

1, 2, 3, he counted in his head. But he lifted the razor away from his arm. Was he really about to cut himself with a razor? This was foolish. He could bleed to death. He could be going mad but he was certain of what he saw.

He stared into his own eyes in the mirror, held the razor tight in his hand again and with a quick strike he sliced it against his arm without breaking his own gaze. Blood splashed across the mirror. "Argh," screamed Clive as the cold steel split through his nerves shooting pain into his brain.

He washed his arm under the cold water. He pulled it away and saw the perfectly straight gash in his arm and the two flaps of skin that had parted on either side. He fainted at the sight of it.

Chapter 6

Clive woke up on the bathroom floor. He could hear the sound of water gushing down the sink. He reached up and shut it off. His head was fuzzy and he felt dizzy. He blinked away the blurriness and stood up.

He saw the red of his own blood splashed on the sink and remembered his arm. The blood had dried painting his forearm burgundy and blocking his view of the skin underneath. He washed away the blood and exposed the ridge of a white scar. He examined the blood stained razor head and touched the edge with his finger feeling its sharpness.

He wiped away the blood from round the sink and cleaned it off the mirror. Some had gone on the carpet so he fetched the cleaner from the kitchen and began scrubbing it clean. It didn't come off and he was out of cleaner. *Lila will kill me if she sees this*, he thought to himself.

He walked to the local store, found a bottle of extra strength carpet cleaner and paid Mo, the old Indian man who ran the shop. He turned to leave the store and two guys barged through him like he wasn't there. One was stocky and bald headed wearing black boots, jeans and a red t shirt, the other was a skinny guy with greasy long hair in a full tracksuit. *A thug and a drug addict*, thought Clive to himself as he decided against saying something.

"Hey Ghandi ," the bald one growled at Mo. "Did you know my granddad used to run a store just like this. He used to give me little presents whenever I visited so to make sure you don't crap on his memory I'm going to take a few things. That ok by you?"

"That is not ok. Leave immediately or I will call the cops," responded Mo as he turned to pick up the phone.

The skinny guy jumped over the counter and yanked the phone away from Mo pulling on the wire so it snapped out of the socket on the wall.

"The police won't help you. They're here to serve Americans," said the bald guy.

Clive shuffled out of the store as quickly as possible. He reached into his pocket to grab his phone and call the cops but there was nothing there. He remembered putting it on the side when he was clearing out the garage and had forgotten to pick it back up when he left the house.

He looked around for something that would help and he saw the carpet cleaner in his bag. He remembered the blood he needs to clean and the miraculously healed cut that led to it.

If he healed quickly then he couldn't get hurt, not for long anyway, and there was nothing to be afraid of in a fight, he reasoned with himself. 'You're a wimp, a coward, a yellow belly, 'Lila's words from the hospital echoed in his head.

He looked up through the store window and saw the skinny guy pushing Mo against the wall. Clive had to do something and fast.

If he was getting in to a fight he didn't these guys to recognise him if they ever bumped into one another in the future. He tore a strip off of the old t-shirt he was wearing, tied it round his face and pulled his hood up.

"Put him down," shouted Clive at the intruders as he burst into the shop.

The bald guy looked at Clive and then went back to helping himself to the shelf of liquor. "We're kinda busy right now so if you want to rob this store, punk, I suggest you come back later," said the bald guy.

"I suggest you put him down," replied Clive, hoping his response sound more witty than cheesy. Clive could feel his leg start to shiver and he shifted his weight trying to pin it down so they wouldn't notice.

"Watch him," said the bald guy to the skinny guy as he let go of Mo and made his way towards Clive. "I've just got to kick this guy's ass then I'll be back."

Before Clive could react the guy was in front of Clive and had swung a punch sending Clive flying backwards through a rack of greetings cards knocking them on to the floor. The bald guy followed it up with a kick, the toe of his booting hitting Clive painfully in the ribs with a loud crack. Clive was sure his ribs were broken.

"Stop, stop," cried Clive rolling on the floor. He'd ran into this fight knowing he could heal any damage but had forgotten about the pain he'd suffer as the damage was made.

"What? I can't hear you," said the thug as he kicked his foot into Clive again.

"I said stop. Please," plead Clive.

The thug swung his leg back again and launched it into Clive but this time Clive caught it and clung on knowing that if he let go it would only be used to beat his already broken ribs. He had to fight back but he'd never been in a real fight in his life. If only he'd thought this through before he ran back into the store.

"Get off," shouted the bald guy hopping around trying to get his leg free.

Clive pulled the guys leg and his badly balanced bulk tumbled down into some shelves, scattering bread on to the floor.

Clive jumped to his knees and quickly jabbed his fist at the guys face as he lay defenceless on the floor. Two sharp blows connected and the bald guy's nose exploded an eruption of blood all over his face.

Clive regretted it. Perhaps he should've run when he had the chance instead of fighting back. Now the guy was angry. Clive jumped to his feet and backed away.

The bald guy clumsily rolled over and flailed around like an upturned tortoise before getting himself to his feet. He wiped his nose across his forearm and looked at the blood. "You're dead," he spat at Clive.

The bald guy ran at Clive knocking him into a display fridge cracking the glass door. Clive got his feet and ran as fast he could around the store with the bloodied bald guy chasing him like a Benny Hill scene directed by Tarantino.

Eventually the bald guy stopped chasing. Clive stood facing him over the top of the island of shelves that stood in the middle of the store. The bald guy went left and Clive followed, then the bald guy went right and Clive copied him again always maintaining the same distance no matter which way round the store he ran.

"You can't run away forever," said the bald guy.

"Just let me go. Please. I'm sorry," said Clive. He'd ran back into the store in instinct hoping to save the poor old guy behind the counter and stop another injustice in this already unjust city but now he was more concerned for his own safety.

The bald guy laughed. "I would've let you go earlier but then you did this," he said pointing to his bloodied nose. "Now I got blood on my shirt and I'm going to get payback from your face."

Clive grabbed a tin from the shelf in front of him and threw it at the bald guy. The bald guy ducked and the tin hit the window behind him cracking the glass.

"Oh you're really pushing it now. I'm going to smash you up so bad your face will look like it was drawn on your neck by an 8 year old."

Clive threw another tin. The bald guy batted it away.

"That's it. Put Ghandi down. You go that way and I'll go this way," he said to his skinny mate who smiled at his friend's instructions showing off a mouth only half filled with brown tombstone teeth.

The men started walking opposite ways round the shelves slowly closing in on Clive. Clive's heart raced, he ran for a small gap next to the skinny guy hoping to push his way through but the skinny guy blocked him and pushed him back towards the bald guy.

Clive climbed the shelves and was about to go over the top when his leg was grabbed by the bald guy who pulled at him to come back down. Clive held on with as tightly as he could as the skinny guy grabbed hold of his other leg and helped pull him down. All three men fell backwards to the floor. A tsunami of groceries covered them moments later as the shelves gave way.

"What have you done to my store you idiot!" screamed Mo the shopkeeper furiously.

Clive got to his feet and ran out the door.

"Come on," the bald guy shouted to his skinny friend as he ran out the door to chase Clive.

Clive got out of store and set off running as fast as his legs would take him down the road. He looked behind him. The bald guy and the skinny guy were following him but he had 20 yards on them by now.

Clive turned the corner and ran into the park hoping to lose them in the maze of paths and bushes in the park. He took as many turns as he could so that he would keep out of sight of his pursuers and jumped through a few of the gaps in the bushes to shortcut his journey. Eventually he made it out the other side of the park, removed his mask and his hood and walked home.

I saved that guy in the store, he thought as he walked home. Alright maybe it wasn't text book hero stuff but it worked. They stopped beating on him and Clive drew them away with the chase. Technically it was a success. Clive felt good, he felt a rush and the liked the way his heart felt fresh like it had a good workout from the rush of adrenaline.

Chapter 7

Clive was busy making tea when Lila got home from work.

"Hey sweetheart. How was work?" asked Clive. He flicked the towel over his shoulder and leant in to taste the ragu in the pan.

"You know. Same old," Lila responded. "What ya cooking?" She walked up behind him, put her arms around his waist and put her head over his shoulder to smell the rising scent from the pan.

"Just spaghetti," said Clive. "Hey, come and watch this."

Clive rolled up his sleeve and took a knife out of the block.

"Where did you get those from?" asked Lila looking at the new scars on his arm.

"Never mind. Watch," said Clive. He aimed the knife at his arm.

"Stop!" screamed Lila grabbing his hand to steady the knife. "What's the matter with you?" Her forehead creased and her jaw hung open.

"Calm down it doesn't hurt," said Clive. He tried to move the knife but Lila gripped his hand tighter.

"Why are you cutting yourself? Is that where those scars are from? How long has this been going on?" Lila reeled off question after question. She couldn't believe her husband had been self harming. How had she not noticed the scars before?

"You need to watch. Then I'll explain," he said holding the knife to his skin again.

"No," said Lila. She took the knife out of his hands. "What's wrong with you Clive? Since when have you been into self-harm?"

"Ok, so maybe the carving knife was a bit extreme but you need to see this. He grabbed a smaller knife he'd been using to cut onions and quickly made a small cut on his forearm before she could stop him.

"Oh my god. Clive stop it, you're scaring me," screamed Lila.

She grabbed the towel from Clive's shoulder and pressed it on to his cut. The white cotton turned red as it soaked up the blood.

Clive let her man handle him around the kitchen, sitting him down on a chair whilst she crouched in front of him keeping pressure on the wound. Clive had a little proud smile on his face because he knew something she didn't.

"Lift it off," he said calmly.

"What?" she asked as a tear rolled down her cheek.

"Lift the towel off my arm and look."

Lila slowly lifted the towel off of his arm. She looked at the cut and rubbed his skin where it had been.

"See," he told her, "Nothing to worry about. I heal almost instantly." He smiled at her expecting to see excitement about his new talent.

"You're such an asshole," she shouted as she walked away from Clive.

"What's wrong?"

"You had me really worried there all for a stupid joke. What was it? Ketchup? Is that what you've been doing with your day? Messing about thinking up sick practical jokes?"

"No seriously I can heal myself. Watch this," said Clive as he picked the big knife Lila had taken off of him and scored slowly down his arm with the tip of the knife. He drew in a sharp breath of air and held his breath as he felt the stinging pain from the cold steel.

The blood ran down over his wrist, along his palm and dripped off the end of his fingertips on to the floor. He put a finger and thumb either side of the wound and pulled it apart, a little drop of blood spurted out. "You see. A real cut. Now watch." He wiped the blood off with the towel to clean the wound and showed it to Lila again as the cut had sealed itself and was slowly fading into a thin white hairline of a scar.

"What the hell was that?" she asked in astonishment. She pressed the palms of her hands on her cheeks distorting her face into an impression of Munch's Scream.

"I told you that I heal myself."

"Seriously how did you do that because if that's another trick I'm going to be mega pissed off."

"It's no trick it just happens."

"Let me see that arm again," Lila said dragging Clive over to the sink to wash off the last traces of blood exposing the roadmap of scars that had started to form on his arm from all his experimental cutting. She rubbed at his arm and scratched her nails on his skin.

"Ow," said Clive.

"We need to get you to a doctor. This is wrong."

"No way. They'll want to experiment on me. I don't want to be a freak show."

"Well we got to do something with it. You're the only person in the world who can heal their skin in a matter of seconds."

"It's not just my skin. Earlier I was sure my ribs were broken but now," Clive patted his chest, "solid as a rock."

"Wait. How did you break your ribs?" asked Lila.

Clive picked up the laptop and showed Lila a news item on the page 'Masked Man Wanted for Criminal Damage'. On the page was a grainy security camera picture of Clive with the mask over his face. "Look," he said showing her the hoody and the torn t-shirt that he'd used as a mask. "I prevented a crime."

"Looks like you caused a crime to me. Why did you smash his shop up?"

"I didn't... Well I did but there were these other two guys who were beating up the owner. I stepped in and saved him. I was a hero."

"So you're a hero now are you?" she asked.

"Yep," he answered proudly.

"A hero with super healing powers? You're a superhero?"

Clive was caught off guard. He'd not thought of it like that before. Maybe he was a real life superhero. Not just some crazy guy in a modified Batman costume but an actual super powered, crime fighting, butt kicking superhero. "I guess I am. Yeah, why not? I'm a superhero," he said proudly to Lila.

"Why not? Because you're a goof ball and I've seen you run away from a moth," she said. "God help anyone who relies on you to save them. Let's hope they're not in a room with a light bulb and an open window at night."

Clive thought about how to explain the changes that had happened to him today. Not the physically ones but the changes in his head. "When we fell into that Hyena enclosure..."

"We didn't fall in Clive you made us go in for a shortcut," Lila cut him off mid-sentence. She still wasn't ready to completely forgive him for that day.

"When we were in there and I couldn't save you it hurt me really bad, more than the wounds, that I couldn't protect my wife. I had to rely on another man to save you. It hurt me Lila," said Clive softly, his voice balancing delicately as he held back his full emotions. The hairs on his forearms rose and he felt a lump in his throat. "With this healing power thing I can change that. Who better to be the bravest guy in the world than the guy who doesn't have to worry about getting hurt? I can just heal myself and if you ever get into trouble again I can save you but if you don't get into trouble then maybe I can save someone else."

"This isn't exactly a tried and tested theory you got here. You've cut yourself a couple of times and it's healed quickly. What if you were stabbed or shot? What if you died? Can you heal being dead?"

"I don't know."

"Well it's kind of a one shot deal because if you can't there's no second go. This isn't one of your video games where you can just hit the reset button and have another go."

"Then I just won't die," Clive snapped at her, annoyed that she wasn't happy with his decision.

Lila spun on her heel and left the room. Clive heard her heavy footsteps as she stomped up the stairs. That usually meant she expected him to follow her.

Clive took the pan off the hob, wiped his hands and followed her up the stairs.

Lila sat in the bedroom on the end of the bed. She had her elbows resting on her knees and her face was in her hands bobbing up and down as she sobbed.

"Hey what's all this about?" Clive asked her in a comforting whisper.

"It's. Just. That. We. Are. Supposed. To be. Trying. For a. Baby," sobbed Lila taking in a big gasp of air in between each word.

"We are trying for a baby."

"No Clive. You want to be a superhero and run around fighting crime. You can't tuck your child into bed at night if you're out catching crooks."

Clive knelt down in front of her so he was looking up at her face. "We can still try for a baby," he said as he pulled her hands away from her face. "And wouldn't it be much better if we had this baby and I knew I could protect it and keep it safe?"

Lila rubbed her fingers down her face wiping away the tears.

"Like the guy in the Audi or the Hyena or anything else that threatens our little family that I've never felt like I could handle. Well, if I can be a superhero then I can handle anything. Even being a dad," said Clive.

Lila looked her husband in the eyes. Clive looked back.

"Let me prove to myself that I can do this Lila. I'll give it up before the baby's born I swear."

Lila sniffed. "Alright then superman," said Lila smiling at her husband. "But you promise me now that you give this up before the baby's born?"

"I promise," he said.

"So what are you going to call yourself then, Super Clive?" she asked.

"The Healer," Clive said mystically waving his arm through the air.

Lila snorted a laugh, "That's lame. How about Superdork?"

"Not funny. I was thinking you know my skin heals so it should be something to do with that."

"Like The Human Band Aid?" Lila laughed.

"How about The Injustice Cure? Because I'm a cure for injustice and I can cure my wounds. It's kind of a double meaning."

"Meh, it works I guess. Hey, you'll need a costume."

"Yeah and a mask," he added.

"Superman doesn't wear a mask and he's really handsome," said Lila.

"Yeah but he supposedly keeps his identity secret with those glasses that Clarke Kent wears. If I put on a pair of glasses now would you not know who I was?"

Lila made her hands into rings and placed them over Clive's eyes. "Hey who is this strange guy in my bedroom. Clive? Clive! We're being robbed," she said loudly and laughed at her own joke.

He pulled her hands away from his face. "Seriously though, if I ever bump into someone I know I don't want them to recognise me. I want them to think I'm some strange guy they've never met."

"I already think you're a strange guy," she laughed. "Let me see what we've got."

Lila opened the wardrobe and threw out clothes into a pile. She bundled them up and handed them to Clive.

"Put these on," she said handing Clive some pants.

"But these are your leggings," he said.

"Most superheroes wear leggings. It gives them better manoeuvrability," she said as she performed a lunge to demonstrate her point.

"I suppose that makes sense," he conceded as he dropped his jeans and stretched the leggings over his legs.

The leggings were too short and stopped halfway up his shins. The top half was tight and Clive felt conscious that his manhood was on display. Lila laughed in hysterics.

"You look a real tool," she said as she reached for her phone to take a picture.

"No," Clive panicked and pulled at the leggings ripping them off.

"Hey I liked those," said Lila.

"Ok seriously now do we have anything that's suitable for a hero to wear?"

Lila looked in the wardrobe again.

"How about these old combats? They're kind of flexible and you can fit lots of crime fighting tools in the pockets," she said handing him the pants.

He put them on and did a few stretches. "Yeah, these work. What about the top."

"I got this. It's black so it matches your pants."

"It's got a picture of a dog on the front," said Clive holding out the black long sleeved t shirt in front of him.

"Yeah. I thought it could be your emblem."

"A dog has nothing to do with The Injustice Cure," he responded pronouncing his new super name in a low pitched, authoritative voice.

"Yeah, your right. We need a good brand for the merchandise. Just put it on inside out for now and I'll keep an eye out for something more suitable when I'm shopping."

"What about the face? I need a mask."

"Well I lent my gimp mask out to a friend so no can do there I'm afraid," she joked.

"I don't want a gimp mask. It needs to be black to go with the rest and so I can hide in the shadows. How about a balaclava?"

"Oooo," said Lila excitedly as she ran off again before returning.

Clive held up the mask she'd handed him. It was a Halloween mask for a black cat. The mask had two eye holes cut out and two ears which stuck out the top.

"I wore it to that Halloween party a couple of years ago. Remember?" said Lila.

"Oh yeah and didn't you wear cat's eye lenses?"

"Good idea. They say that the eyes are the most recognisable aspect of a person's face. If you cover those up no one will ever suspect it's you. Go put them on and let's see the full outfit."

Clive trudged into the bathroom and returned shortly. He had on black combat trousers with a couple of pockets bulging full, a black long sleeved t shirt with the outline of dog still visible from the inside and the tag hanging out at the back. On his head was the cat's mask, the ears taped down with band aids and yellow slitty eyes looking out from the eyeholes.

Lila bit her lip to try and stifle the laugh. "What have you got in your pockets?" she asked pointing to the bulges in his combat pants.

Clive opened one pocket and took out the contents. "Some scissors and a pen knife in case I need to pick a lock or cut through rope or something," he closed that pocket and opened the other, "some bandages, disinfectant and pain killers in case I need to treat somebody's wounds."

Lila couldn't hold it in and laughed out loud as she fell backwards on to the bed.

"Right, you're not taking this seriously," Clive said as he turned to go back out of the room.

Lila skipped across and grabbed his arms. "I am. You look really good," she said. "I think we may need to get you a different t shirt and perhaps lose the cat mask though."

Clive pulled the mask off of his head. "Yeah this is lame but it will do for tonight."

"Tonight?" asked Lila.

"Yeah. I'm serious about this. I'm going out tonight," said Clive.

"Why don't you wait until you've got the full kit?"

"Crime waits for no man," he said cheesily.

Lila stared blankly at him.

"I'm not changing my mind Lila. I'm doing this," he told her.

"I know you are baby, but tonight is one of my windows. You know, ovulation for the nation," she said, winking at him on the last word.

"I can do that before I leave," he said and pushed her on to the bed.

Chapter 8

Clive had been on patrol as Shoreline City's new hero for four nights now and had yet to see any actual crime. The first night Clive was glad nothing happened as his nerves had gotten the better of him and he spent most of the night throwing up his Bolognese. On the second night he told himself was ready for trouble but really hoped there was none, by the third night he was growing restless but now, on the fourth night, he was beginning to think that maybe this whole idea was stupid.

He'd improved his costume at least. Now if he did have to fight crime he wouldn't look so stupid. Gone was the cat mask replaced with a balaclava. The inside out t-shirt had also been replaced with one of the skin tight black Lycra tops that athletes wear. Clive didn't like the usual guys that wore this kind of top in public, they were the athletic ones who wore it as though it was a badge of honour knowing it was only for the super lean as even the slightest bit of flabbiness would show up. Since Clive had recovered from the attack he'd joined that club and the top clung to his lean torso.

He had gained a few new tools as well, to go in the many pockets of his combat pants. A torch, for obvious reasons, a water bottle, again obvious, duct tape and cable ties for restraining any criminals and a rape alarm in case he got into trouble he couldn't get out of. Lila had insisted on that last one. Clive figured he could hand it out to the first damsel in distress he rescues.

He'd decided to go patrol down in the park near the hospital. He'd read that the night staff were often mugged and attacked on their way home from work through the park. He stuck to the shadows as usual hoping his all black costume would keep him invisible and used the bushes for extra cover.

The first people he saw were a group of boys who'd gotten hold of some beer and were drinking it in the park. Clive reasoned that they weren't causing any real trouble and perhaps it also wouldn't be wise to take on that many people on his first night. Anyway he wanted to be a cool hero and confiscating alcohol from minors wasn't exactly going to achieve that. Especially when it went viral after one of them would no doubt upload a video of him being beaten up by kids.

He skulked about some more, diving for cover in the bushes as a young woman made her way through the park. He kept well hidden but when she sped up to walk past him he figured she knew he was there.

He wondered what would be said of him if people knew he was hiding in bushes in a dark park in the middle of the night. Would they believe his story or would he be branded a perverted peeping tom?

He'd nearly done a full sweep of the park and was preparing himself for another eventless night when he decided to check out the subway that ran under the road and separated the park from the hospital.

He heard a scuffling and pressed himself in tight against the wall at the entrance of the subway. He listened carefully hoping in the back of his mind that it was just rats or some other nocturnal animal. Then the scuffling was replaced by grunting and the sound of a struggle followed by the panicked cries of a woman.

Clive ran through the subway towards the source of the noise and came out on to the scene of a man pulling at a woman's bag. The bag was wrapped round the woman's arm and every time the thief pulled at it he pulled the woman with it, dragging her along the floor.

Clive continued his run and leapt as high as he could off the ground with a Bruce Lee style kung fu kick. He'd never done any sort of martial arts in his life but for some reason it felt the natural instinctive thing for him to do.

The kick landed on the guys arm and Clive fell to the floor probably hurting more than the recipient of the kick.

The thief ran off and Clive pulled himself to his feet to give chase.

"Please don't leave me," sobbed the woman at Clive.

He looked down at her. She was a young woman probably not much older than Clive. Her top had been ripped at the shoulder where the thief had been trying to pull her handbag away. Her tights were laddered and full of holes. Her mascara was painting zebra stripes down her cheeks.

"Don't leave me alone," she sobbed again.

Clive helped her to her feet. "It's ok," he said, "you're safe now."

The woman leant forward into Clive's chest. He put his arms round her to comfort her and felt the dampness of her tears through his thin Lycra shirt.

"Are you hurt?" Clive asked.

"No. I'll be ok," she replied.

"We should take you to the hospital, get you checked over."

"No I'm ok really. I just want to get home. Will you walk me to my car?"

It suddenly dawned on Clive that no part of his costume masked his voice.

"Who are you?" asked the woman.

"I'm The Injustice Cure," said Clive in the most gravely, deep voice he could manage trying to sound butch and manly.

"Well Injustice Cure. I'm Charlotte, thanks for saving me."

"It was nothing. Where there is injustice in Shoreline City then there is The Injustice Cure," said Clive in his new superhero voice trying to explain the meaning of the name but then instantly regretting the corniness of his words and the obviousness of the statement.

"Yeah, I get it," Charlotte smiled. "What's with the cat's eyes?"

"It's to keep my identity secret."

Through the makeup dripping down her face Clive could see pretty features. She had big plump cushiony lips and bright round eyes that reminded him of the type that they give to Japanese cartoon characters. She was pretty, exactly Clive's type, and he couldn't stop staring at her. The ripped top that exposed her pale skin shoulder wasn't helping either. Clive kept thinking of that thing they say about the movies, *the hero defeats the bad guy and gets the girl*. He remembered Lila and gave himself a mental slap round the face.

"Well, this is me," she said swinging her car keys in the air and snapping Clive out of his fantasy. "I think I'm safe from here."

"Ok no problem," he said.

"Thanks again. I can't tell you how grateful I am for you saving me back there. You're a real hero. This world needs more people like you and I can sleep safer knowing this city is being watched by the Crime Cure."

"The Injustice Cure," Clive corrected her.

"The Injustice Cure. Sorry."

An awkward moment filled the air as neither of them knew what to say next. In the movies this time is when the superhero vanishes in to thin air but Clive didn't want to leave her. Those dewy round eyes longed for him to protect her.

"Here, have this rape alarm in case you're attacked again," he said to her holding out the little black plastic box.

"Already got one," she said patting her handbag.

"Then how about I give you my number just case you get into trouble again?" he told her. After he said it he realised he'd offered out his personal details. That was a mistake.

"Really? My own superhero to call on when I want? Every girls dream." She pulled her phone out of her handbag, unlocked it and held it in front of her. The camera flashed photographing Clive. "For the contact picture," she explained as she handed him the phone.

He entered his number and pressed save before handing the phone back. She opened her bag and looked into it as she dropped her phone inside. Clive took his opportunity and set off running hoping to be out of sight before she looked up. He failed and cringed at how stupid he must look as she watched him sprinting away into the night.

Chapter 9

Clive walked in the door kicked his boots off and slumped down on the couch. He pulled his balaclava off his head and sighed. He regretted how he left it with Charlotte, partly because he was married and shouldn't have given her his number and partly because he'd ran away like an idiot. *It was typical Clive*, he thought to himself, half committed to something but too scared to follow it through.

"Another fail?" asked Lila surprising him as she approached from behind.

"Nope, nothing," he said jumping up from the couch like Lila had caught him thinking about Charlotte.

"Alright jumpy. I was just asking. Are you gonna call it quits now then?"

"I saved a woman from being mugged tonight," he said.

"Really, that's good. Why the sigh then?"

"It still just didn't feel enough. A concerned passer-by could have done what I did tonight. I need to do more something that's a full use of my powers. Something big," he said.

"Big crime doesn't happen every night and it's still early days in your crime fighting career. It will come. Anyway tonight sounded like a good way to pop the cherry. Tell me more."

"Nothing much to say really, I saw a woman being attacked so I went over and the guy ran off."

"Did you chase him?"

"No the woman was upset she didn't want me to leave her and she looked all vulnerable on the floor with a ripped top and messy makeup. I had to help her."

"She had a ripped top? Was he raping her?" Lila asked with an even mix of concern and intrigue.

"No. It was just how her bag was round her shoulder. It was tangled in her top and when he pulled it must've broken the strap of her top."

"Oh ok," said Lila disappointed that it wasn't juicier than it was. "So were her boobs out?"

"Nah not really. I mean you could see like the top of one of them but no nipple."

Lila punched Clive in the arm getting her bony knuckles deep into the gap between his bicep and his triceps in the way only she knew how.

"Ouch what was that for?" he asked.

"You know what," she said. "Was she attractive?"

"Yeah," answered Clive instantly realising the trap he'd just walked into.

"Oh, so that's the kind of superhero you are is it? Saving the pretty ones so you can have a closer look at their boobs?" she asked.

"No that's not how it was. I didn't look. Honestly."

"Chill out. I'm just messing with you," said Lila. "Was she our age?"

"No she was a little bit older, more of a milf."

Lila punched Clive again.

This time Clive smiled. He was enjoying making her jealous, payback for the time she went to dinner with the zoo keeper. At the same time though he felt a little guilty because he had been attracted to this woman and thought things that a married man probably shouldn't.

"I can't help it if beautiful women need my help. If it was a fat, bald, ugly dude I would have still saved him."

"You don't have to enjoy it so much," she pouted. "So what happened after the mugger ran off."

"She was really grateful and kept thanking me and asked me to walk her to her car."

"And did you?"

"Of course I did. It was dark, she was alone. It was the right thing to do."

"What did you talk about when you walked her to her car?"

"Not much she just kept thanking me telling me how I was her hero and that she would sleep better knowing I was out on the streets protecting her."

"Slut," hissed Lila.

Clive laughed at Lila's jealousy.

Lila stood up swiftly. "I'm going to bed," she said as she walked towards the door. She stopped in the doorway, "maybe I'll sleep better knowing you're here to protect me," she said in a mocking girly voice.

Clive chuckled and followed her to bed.

Chapter 10

It was time to head back out for another night of crime fighting. Clive finished his coffee hoping the caffeine would be enough of a kick to keep him awake all night and headed out of the door in his all black crime fighting outfit.

His rescue of Charlotte had been just the motivation he needed to carry on his mission and now he was ready for something bigger.

Tonight was Saturday night and that meant the city would be full of the party crowd and, Clive hoped, the fighting, drugs and prostitution that goes with the less savoury side of it.

He started his night hiding out on the rooftops opposite one of the busiest clubs in the city, Hybrid.

He waited there for hours watching the queue for the club slowly move forward. This wasn't how he imagined his life as a superhero. In the movies the crime just always seems to be right there in front of the hero. They didn't show all this waiting around, bored, cold and tired.

Eventually a smart black car pulled up outside the club covered in shiny chrome that twinkled as it reflected the neon lights of the bar. Clive picked up his binoculars hoping it was some action.

A man got out of the passenger side. He was wearing a black leather jacket and had long hair tied into a ponytail. The man walked up to the bouncers and shook hands with them. They were talking and the bouncers laughed at whatever the man was saying before letting him straight into the club.

Clive put the binoculars down, it was most likely the club owner. Who else would be able to park right outside and stroll in like that? Sure enough a few minutes later the man came back out, jumped back in the car and it drove off.

Clive yawned and checked his watch, 4 hours he'd been lying on that roof now and he could feel his eyes getting heavy. It was time to move on.

He climbed down from the roof and, using a back alley for cover, he made his way to one of the smaller nightclubs,

Lithium. Clive had been there once when he'd gone out drinking with some of the guys from his office. He hadn't liked it. The carpets were dirty and sticky, there was a funny smell and everyone in the place stared at you as you entered like you were a gunslinger walking into a saloon in the Wild West. For criminals though this must be like a honey pot to a badger.

He crouched behind a dumpster that was a few metres down from the entrance and tried to come up with a plan for getting to the action inside. Whilst he was weighing up the idea of climbing in the restroom window he heard the doors of the club slam open and the sounds of a struggle.

Clive stood up and peered over the dumpster. Two men had tumbled out of the club and were scuffling on the ground. A handful of other men clutching beer bottles were stood around cheering and shouting.

The two fighting men were drunk and their wild swings were missing their target or landing so weakly that the recipient didn't even flinch. At one point one of them missed so badly he swung his whole body round 360 degrees and corkscrewed down on to the floor. This fight was weak and a few of the spectators got bored of watching and went back inside. Eventually one of the men got fed up and walked off leaving the other sat on the floor swaying from side to side.

Clive wondered whether this was even a crime it was that pathetic. Even pre-superpowers Clive would have stood a chance against those guys.

Clive was despondent and walked away not even bothering to hide in the shadows. *Another night and another waste of time,* he thought to himself.

He'd only been walking a few minutes when the black car drove past him again. He turned and watched as it went by. Something niggled at the base of neck about that car, maybe he had a crime radar as part of his new powers. He followed it and found himself back at Lithium. By the time Clive got himself set in his hiding place the ponytailed man was coming back out of the club and getting in to the car again.

The car set off and Clive knew he had to follow it. He started running and, to his surprise, he was fast, much faster than he remembered ever being able to run. Although he wasn't as fast as the car he was able to keep it in his sights, ducking and weaving under the canopies of the closed stores and catching up lost ground when the car stopped at the lights.

He followed the car for 3 miles before it came to a stop in the parking lot of a hardware store. Clive hid behind some bushes that bordered the lot and watched the car. It was parked there for 4 minutes before a rusty old red ford pulled alongside it. Both cars had lowered their windows and were discussing something.

Clive wasn't near enough to hear so he tiptoed round to the back of the black car keeping as low as possible. His stomach churned as he thought about being caught and what might happen if he was.

"Lithium needs more stock of brown and take some of the white stuff down to Hybrid," said the voice from the black car. The guy sounded like a bad mafia film.

"Yeah alright," replied the man in the red car. "You got any more samples boss? I got a guy interested in buying some stock."

"What did I tell you about doing business? You're just an errand boy. You don't talk to no one about supplies or nothing unless I tell you to. You hear me?" shouted the angry voice of the man in the black car.

"Yes boss."

"I got enough on my plate trying to keep the heat off me without you telling more people my business."

Clive knew he'd stumbled on to real crime at last, a drugs deal. He started getting nervous and his left leg trembled like jelly struggling to hold his balance.

He realised that they would have at least one gun, probably a gun each. Lila's words rang through his head. She'd warned him he didn't know just how strong he was and what he could and couldn't heal. He should have bought a bulletproof vest. Why didn't he buy a bulletproof vest?

His worrying was interrupted by red and blue lights bouncing off the store windows and flooding the small parking lot. It was the cops.

The black car sped away leaving Clive exposed in the open of the parking lot. Clive looked up at the guy in the red car who in his panic had shut the engine off and was a sitting duck for the cops. Clive ducked back to the bushes.

The police skidded their car to a stop and jumped out with their pistols drawn aimed at the driver of the red car.

They hadn't noticed the black car speeding away. The black car was the one containing the kingpin of this deal and Clive knew catching him would have a bigger impact on the illegal drug market of Shoreline City. He wanted to tell the cops that they need to follow the black car but they had their guns drawn and were a little jumpy trying to get their guy into cuffs. This wasn't the time to surprise them from the bushes.

Clive set off running as fast as he could in the direction of the black car. In the background he could hear the disappearing voices of the shouting policemen.

The black car was out of sight. Clive ran down the middle of the road, looking for evidence of the black car and checked left and right down every side street.

He reached the intersection with Main Street and saw the red glow of taillights in the distance to his left. He turned and picked up his pace running at such a speed that the white lines painted on the dark black tarmac of the road beneath his feet were just a blur. He felt out of control, his legs moving faster than he could consciously control them.

Clive was catching the car faster than he thought but then realised the car was parked at the side of the road with the engine running. Clive ran to the driver's door, yanked out the driver and punched him square in the face. Clive heard a cracking sound as the driver's nose broke and blood ran down his neck bleeding into the white collar his crisp shirt. The guy was out cold so Clive dropped him and ran round to the passenger side.

The door was locked and inside he could see the pony tailed crook fumbling with the glove compartment.

Clive smashed the window with his elbow and raked out some of the glass. The muzzle of a pistol poked out at Clive and he ducked just in time as the sound of the shot echoed of the buildings. Clive's ears were ringing from being so close to the gunshot but he couldn't stay still. He crawled on his knees round the other side of the car as the pony tailed man got out, his gun in his hand looking for Clive.

"Come here you freak," growled the man.

Clive scuttled sideways like a crab along the opposite side of the car.

"You messed with the wrong guy. I'm gonna make you pay," said the man who was trying to see over the hood and find Clive.

Clive had reached the back of the car now and pressed his back against the trunk. A little bit of sick jumped into his mouth and Clive swallowed it down quickly, the bile burned as it slid back down his throat.

Clive was scared. He thought about making a run for it but knew he'd be shot in the back before he made it more than 5 yards. Clive needed to get to the man and disarm him but the man had all angles from the car covered, all except one. Clive dropped on to his belly and crawled under the car. It was a tight squeeze and the heat from the exhaust burned his skin and healed instantly under Clive's powers. He crawled silently all the way to the front of the car.

"Come on sucker. You're not so tough now are you?" asked the man still pointing his gun into thin air.

Clive was under the engine and inches from the man's feet. He reached out grabbed the man's ankles and yanked hard sending the guy tumbling down backwards on to the ground and landing with a heavy thump. The gun had come out of his hand and was lying two feet away on the road.

Clive slid out from under the car as fast as he could but in the same time the pony tailed man had grabbed the gun and was aiming it at Clive.

Clive lunged at him as a shot was fired. The bullet hit Clive in his left shoulder passing right through his flesh and out the other side, spinning his body round and dropping him to the floor. He regained his feet quickly and went back at the man grabbing the front of his suit, pushing him backwards over and on to the ground. Clive slammed the man into the ground, smashing his head into the tarmac. He repeatedly lifted the man's body off the ground and slammed him down again watching his head snap forward each time as his skull impacted with the black top. After a while the man's body went limp in Clive's hands and he let go.

Clive stood up and put his hand to his shoulder, the pain was excruciating and unbearable. It was just a flesh wound and had begun to heal already. He had been lucky this time.

He picked the guy up, threw him over his shoulder and carried him all the way back to the cops in the store car park. On the way he played the scene over in his mind. 'The Injustice Cure saves the day' would be the headline. Clive would be a hero and Lila would see how good he had done. It wasn't enough though, this was just the start. Fear had driven Clive when he beat the dealer not bravery. He still needed to conquer his fear.

"You missed one," Clive said throwing the pony tailed drug dealer to the floor in front of the officer.

The officer looked at the blood on Clive's costume. It took the overweight, Chief Wiggums look-a-like officer a good few seconds to react before he drew his weapon and pointed it at Clive.

"Stay where you are!" he ordered. "Hands in the air."

The other officer who had been securing the errand boy in the back of the police car heard the commotion and jumped out with his gun drawn as well. Now Clive was flanked by guns aimed at him.

"Easy guys," said Clive raising his hands. "I'm on your side."

"Get down on the ground!" shouted the officer again.

Clive dropped to his knees. It couldn't be over so soon. He'd just busted his first major crime and now he was going to be identified and no doubt charged with some offence. His crime fighting career was over before it had even begun.

"Hands on your head," said Chief Wiggums.

Clive did as he was ordered. The officer slowly circled around Clive until he was behind him, stepped forward and when he reached for the cuffs on his belt, Clive struck, turning in a flash, taking the officer's gun and pointing it at him whilst he used the officer as a shield between himself and the other gun.

"Look I'm on your side. I don't want this to turn nasty. I caught your drug dealer so just let me go," Clive pleaded with them.

"You're only making things harder for yourself," shouted the other officer who was now crouched behind his patrol car.

"Yeah you scumbag, freakoid, asshole I'll get you for this," snarled the sweating lump of lard that Clive held as a hostage.

"I'm just going to back away slowly and then let you go," instructed Clive.

"I'll catch you and when I do I'll make you pay for this," said Chief Wiggums. Clive was surprised at how nasty this guy was considering he had a gun pointed in his back. This wasn't the picture of the grateful cop, fighting side by side with him against crime that he had imagined.

Clive backed slowly to towards the bushes that bordered the parking lot and nearer to the shadows of the back alleys that would hide him. As he neared the kerb the fat officer struggled in his grip trying to spin out of Clive's arms and grab the gun back but he wasn't anywhere near agile enough and he struggled, pulling on one end of the gun whilst Clive held the other.

"Shoot him," shouted the fat officer to the thin one.

The sound of a bullet being fired ricocheted through the air and the fat officer dropped to the floor holding his knee. He'd been shot and Clive knew when an officer has been shot anyone involved was in for a hard time.

He took his opportunity and disappeared into the shadows of the night.

Chapter 11

Clive ran around the city, ducking and diving down alleyways trying to make as many turns as possible just in case he was being tailed by the police. Eventually he found his way to the edge of the mountains and an old tin shed. He sat down clumsily in the dry dirt behind it, rattling the rusty metal wall as he tried to shield himself out of view from the road.

His phone rang. He didn't recognise the number.

"Hello."

"Hey. This is Charlotte. The girl you saved from the other night," said the voice at the other end of the phone.

"Oh… Oh," said Clive changing into his deep superhero voice.

Charlotte giggled at the other end of the line. Clive smiled.

"What can I do for you Charlotte?" he asked.

"Erm, this may sound weird but did you just run by my apartment?"

"I've been doing a lot of running tonight. What's your location?" Clive was trying his best to sound like an authority figure and was using words he'd heard used by cops and senior military figures in films.

"It's on the Coast Road. Opposite the gas station."

"Yes I was just in that vicinity."

"Are you fighting crime," she asked excitedly.

"Ma'am, I'm The Injustice Cure. I'm always fighting crime because crime never sleeps." Clive cringed at that one. Perhaps he'd gone a bit too far with this cop language.

"Oh," said Charlotte sounding impressed. "Did you catch him?"

"Affirmative. That's one less drug dealer on the streets of Shoreline City," he said proudly as he imagined how brave Charlotte must be thinking he is.

"You're so brave," she said. "A girl could make use of a good man like you."

"Really, how so?" said Clive dropping his guard, forgetting about the cop talk and his superhero disguised voice.

Charlotte giggled again. "Hey if you're not fighting more crime tonight you're welcome to stop by. I just made some cookies."

"That's against protocol ma'am but for you I think I can make an exception. What's your precise location?" asked Clive.

"Opposite the gas station, in the old Brook Building. My apartment's on the top floor."

"I'll be there as soon as I'm able," said Clive.

"OK. See you soon, Injustice Cure."

Clive put his phone back in his pocket. He was grinning widely and his heart felt light as air.

He set off walking towards Charlotte's apartment when Lila came into his mind. What was he doing going to see another woman for cookies? *That sounds like a euphemism*, he thought to himself. He was The Injustice Cure, saviour of the city. It was his duty to make its citizens feel safe, that's all he was doing nothing else. He knew he was only kidding himself and he remembered how he felt when Lila went for dinner with Brian. He thought about her feeling the same emotions he did if she found out he was visiting Charlotte. He promised himself he would just say hi, take a cookie and leave.

Clive reached Lila's apartment building. It was a box shaped, red brick building. An old one but not old enough for it to be classic, more of a mid-life crisis building in need of a makeover.

He decided he'd make a real superhero entrance by going up the fire escape and through the window. He went round the side of the building and saw that the fire escape was a good 15 feet off the ground. *They make this look so easy in the movies*, thought Clive to himself as he struggled to reach the bottom of the rusting iron ladder. He pulled a dumpster nearer and climbed on top of it, then jumped on to the ladder and pulled himself up.

He climbed the stairs up to the top floor and peered in the window. Charlotte was inside getting changed. Clive saw a glimpse of her lace knickers before she slipped her nightie down over her body. He jumped back from the window edge. He felt his cheeks burn as he blushed.

He sat there for a few minutes not wanting to knock on the window straight after she got changed because she'll know he saw her. He wanted to pretend he arrived after she got dressed.

He waited until a few minutes passed then knocked on the window. Charlotte opened the window and he jumped in.

"Oh my god what happened to you?" she asked seeing the bullet hole in his shirt.

"It's nothing," said Clive deciding against continuing his cop talk in person.

Charlotte put her hand to his wound and ran her fingers over it. "Does it hurt?" she asked.

"Nah," he answered.

"You're so brave," she said as she ran her hand from the wound down his chest and then his stomach before letting it fall away at his belt. "You hungry?" she asked walking into her kitchen.

"I wasn't before but now I've smelt those cookies," he answered.

"How many do you want?"

"One's enough, I gotta watch my weight. Can't be fighting crime with a belly."

"You look lean enough to me," said Charlotte with a wink.

Clive smiled bashfully.

"Mmmm. Looks good," said Clive trying to break the tension in the room.

Charlotte handed him the plate and their hands touched. He looked at her face and their eyes locked in a gaze both of them trying guess what the other would do next.

Charlotte moved closer to Clive without breaking eye contact. Clive licked his lips and blinked. Charlotte leant in to him and kissed him softly on the lips. For a moment Clive kissed her back. Then he pulled away.

"I can't do this," he said. He dropped the plate of cookies on the floor. The plate smashed as it hit the hard floorboards. He turned and jumped back of the window and into the street.

Clive started running back home. It wasn't until he'd ran a couple of blocks that he realised he was smiling. The smile soon dropped and guilt kicked in. He was married. Not just married he was starting a family. How could he bring a child into a relationship where he couldn't even remain faithful?

He slowed his run to a walk to give himself more time to think before he got home. Lila had become more and more pushy lately. She was obsessed with having a baby and sometimes Clive thought she had settled for him just because she wanted a baby so badly. It was like Clive was just a third party in her desire to have a baby as quickly as possible, a means to an end. She'd never once asked him if he was ready or if he even wanted a baby. She was just concerned with her own needs.

He started wondering whether he did love her or was he just happy that he had a woman who was quite clearly out of his league. Either way, they could not keep trying for a child until he decided.

Chapter 12

Clive walked into the house and went straight to the bathroom. He had to peel his shirt off where the dried blood had stuck it to his body. He washed the blood off his chest and inspected the scar on his shoulder. It wasn't a pretty one and the skin had puckered up around the entry hole making it look like a cat's bum.

He splashed cold water on to his face and stared himself in the mirror. The cat's eye lenses he was still wearing stared back at him like a stranger. Not the confrontation dodging, yellow bellied meek Clive Silver, husband of Lila Silver, but a battle hardened, restorer of justice, fighting crime and tipping the balance of fairness back in favour of the honest. He wondered which one of these men had kissed Charlotte. It was a dangerous thought and he cast her out of his mind as quickly as he could.

Clive imagined what it would be like back in the hyena enclosure now that he had his powers. It would have been him that saved Lila and not that pony tailed, crap shovelling, baby koala stealer. It would have been Clive that Lila looked upon as the brave saviour of her life. Instead he had Charlotte as his doting fan.

Lila walked in to the bathroom and, seeing Clive's bare, toned chest, she wrapped her arms around him from behind and kissed his neck.

"Take those things out. They give me the freaks," she said in his ear.

He pinched his fingers over his eyes and slipped the lenses back into their case.

"That better?" He said turning round to face her with his own brown eyes and putting his hands on her waist.

"Yes," she said softly before kissing him on the lips.

He looked into her eyes and smiled. He'd been assessing her all night, wondering if it was a mistake marrying her and now, after one kiss, he knew it wasn't a mistake. Still, Charlotte wouldn't leave his thoughts.

"What's that?" She pointed to his new scar.

"It's nothing don't worry," he dismissed her leaning in to kiss her again.

She moved away avoiding his kiss. "It looks like a bullet hole. Have you been shot?"

"It's not that bad. It's healed already."

"It's not that bad. What if it had been your head or your heart? Would it have healed then? You need to think about this Clive. I need you alive."

A tear rolled down Lila's cheek. Clive wasn't used to seeing her looking vulnerable. She was always so much stronger than him. She was always the one pulling him into line, bossing him around, telling him what to do and being brave for both of them.

"I'm not going to die. I'll make sure of it." Clive hugged her tight to his chest, her arms folding in front of her between their bodies as he squeezed her gently. The protective instinct of The Injustice Cure was bleeding into the personality of Clive Silver.

She rested her head on his shoulder and whispered, "I love you."

"I love you too," he said stroking her hair.

She pulled away from him, ripped off a couple of sheets of toilet paper and wiped her tears. "There's something we need to talk about," she said.

Clive felt his heart jump as though someone had squeezed it in their palm. His hairs stand on end. How could she know? Was it his body language, lipstick on his lips or the smell of another woman on his clothes?

"What is it?" he asked apprehensively.

She grabbed his arms and switched places with him, sitting him down on the toilet lid. "You know how we've been trying and the doctor's said that nature will take its course?"

Clive's felt his heart speed up as more of the nervous chemical sped round his blood stream heating up his body and sweating his palms. "Yeah," he answered.

"Well nature has taken its course," she said. The corners of her mouth flickered as she struggled to contain a smile.

He let out the lungful of air he was holding. "What d'ya mean?"

"I missed my period," she said excitedly almost jumping off her feet.

"Does that mean you're pregnant," asked Clive cautiously not knowing whether the change in Lila's body was something to celebrate or worry about. He'd never fully understood all this cycle's business, nor did he ever have any interest in finding out.

"Well it might just be that I'm late but I'm usually bang on time. So yes, that means I'm pregnant."

"OK," he said. His mind raced with the thoughts he'd had on his way home. How he'd just told himself he can't raise a child in this relationship. Not yet anyway, not until he made his mind up. Now his mind had been made up for him. No more Charlotte. No more doubts. Put everything he could into this relationship, this pregnancy. Make it work. Don't be a screw up dad.

"Aren't you happy?" asked Lila, her eyebrows making a v shape of agitation.

"Of course I am. It's what we wanted, isn't it?"

"Well it's what I wanted, but by the look and sound of you I'm not so sure it's what you wanted," she said as she scowled at him.

"No. I do want this. I want this so much. We can be a family at last," he reassured her.

She sat on his knee and cuddled him, wiggling her body in excitement. "This superhero thing has to stop though. I'm not raising a bastard," she said with her arms still around him.

Clive's phone rang. He lifted Lila off his knee and stood up to retrieve it from his pocket. He checked the screen, unknown number.

"Hello," he said.

Lila could hear a women's voice from the other end but couldn't make out what she was saying.

Clive's face lit up as he heard the voice, it was Charlotte's.

"Yes this is The Injustice Cure how can I help?" he said in his deep, gravelly superhero voice.

Lila looked at him puzzled at the voice he put on. He lifted his finger to his lip to shush her.

"Ok wait there. I'll be right over," he said ending the call.

"Who was that?" asked Lila.

"It was Charlotte, the woman I saved in the park."

"She has your number?" said Lila angrily.

"This isn't the time. She's in trouble. A guy's following her. I need to help her."

Chapter 13

Clive tiptoed through the car park.

"Charlotte. Charlotte," he said in a whispered shout.

Charlotte ran out from the shadows and pressed herself into Clive's chest sobbing.

"I didn't know what to do. When you left I tried to catch up with you to apologise, then this guy started following me and I ran," she blubbed to him.

"Shhh, its ok I'm here now," he responded in his butch hero voice. "Where is he?"

"I think he ran into the zoo when he heard you coming. Oh Injustice Cure I thought he was going to kill me," she sobbed.

"Stick near me. We're going to find him and cure this injustice," he said puffing out his chest.

He padded across the parking lot as fast as he could go and stopped by the entrance to allow Charlotte to catch up.

"We've got to go over the top. I'll help you," he said to her.

Clive jumped and pulled himself up on to the wall before leaning over and pulling Charlotte up as well. He lowered her back down the other side gently before jumping down himself. Clive's stomach twisted as he saw the picture of the hyena on the large map displayed on the board in the zoo's entrance.

"Over there," he pointed at a small building across the courtyard where a light shone through the blinds.

"I don't want to go in there," Charlotte said.

"OK. You hide, I'll go."

Clive swiftly moved across the courtyard, his feet barely touching the ground. He stood in front of the door to the building, drew in a deep breath and burst through the doors.

The inside of the building had 2 long rows of benches running down either side of its length. On the benches were various bits of scientific equipment. Clive slowly walked down the building passing an incubator full of small round, ping pong ball sized eggs, a tray full of test tubes of a brown muddy liquid, a whiteboard with the dietary requirements for a tiger scribbled on it and other science stuff that someone might use to look after animals in a zoo.

He reached the end of the benches and heard a noise coming from a small room off the end. Clive looked at the thick door of the room and temperature readout above it, it was a fridge. He was afraid of being locked inside, not a nice way to go, so he crouched down behind a stainless steel trolley and waited for the occupant of the room to come out.

Clive heard the tinkling of fragile glass gently banging together as the man emerged clutching a little wooden rack of test tubes.

Clive pounced and pinned him down, glass tubes of liquids smashed to the floor. Clive paused for a second worrying that perhaps he's attacked a scientist working late at the zoo. He hadn't even stopped to check this was the attacker. The man had a grizzly brown lumberjack beard with specks of grey in it and was wearing a brown leather jacket. *This isn't a scientist,* thought Clive.

He rolled the man over on to his front and pinned him down by putting his knee on the man's neck. Clive took a cable tie from the pocket of his combat pants and zipped the man's wrists together tight.

"What are you doing?" protested the man without panic or fear in his voice.

Clive stood over him, "Shut up you sick pervert," he growled but not with his superhero voice this was Clive's own voice, deep with anger and loathing for this sex pest.

Clive pulled the man to his feet and strapped him to a chair.

"You're making a mistake. I'm not who you think I am," he protested some more, his voice still unflustered by the experience.

Clive ran out leaving the man sat alone in the chair.

"Charlotte, I got him," he said looking into the shadows for movement. "Charlotte," Clive called again with no response. *Damn,* he thought as he contemplated the fact that he might have just tied up an innocent guy whilst the real attacker was out here making off with Charlotte.

"I'm here," said a voice from the shadows and Charlotte skipped out. "Did you get him?" she asked.

"Yeah he's inside."

Charlotte leant forward and kissed Clive's balaclava clad cheek. He wished the balaclava wasn't there so he could feel her lips on his skin again.

"You're my hero," she said to him as she grabbed his hand and led him towards the building where the man was being held captive.

They walked inside to see the man struggling to free himself.

"Is that the guy?" asked Clive.

"Oh Injustice Cure, please don't let him hurt me," she said in a high pitched voice as she wrapped her arms round Clive's neck and pushed her face into his chest.

Clive reached round and rubbed her back in small circles between her shoulder blades. "It's ok. You're safe. I've tied him up and I won't let anyone hurt you."

"Oh, I don't know what I'd do without you," she gushed like the damsel in distress from an old black and white film.

"Don't listen to her. You don't know the truth," shouted the man in the chair.

"Oh Injustice Cure, make him stop. Please make him be quiet," she said as a tear rolled down her left cheek and into the corner of her mouth.

Clive got angry that someone was upsetting Charlotte, pulled the duct tape from his pocket and tore off a length.

"Oh for Christ's sake, don't do that," said the man as he moved his head around trying to avoid the tape. He wasn't successful and Clive stuck the tape over his mouth.

"What happens now?" asked Charlotte.

"We hand him over to the police. Let him serve his time in prison."

"The police!" exclaimed Charlotte, "But they're just a set of overpaid, incompetent, admins. You know as well as I do that he'll be back out within 24 hours. In fact he'll probably be the one who's filing charges against you."

In his head Clive knew she was telling the truth. His experience with the cops earlier that night was evidence enough that they wouldn't just accept a prisoner being handed to them and, after that officer was shot, they would no doubt have it in for Clive.

"Kill him Clive," said the voice inside his head. It was the deep Nigerian voice again. Clive shook his head a couple of times hoping to dislodge it.

"Are you ok?" asked Charlotte.

The man in the chair struggled against his restraints and made muffled noises through the tape. His face was shiny with perspiration.

"Yeah I'm fine," he said to her smiling through the mouth hole of his balaclava.

"Clive. The man, he needs to die," said the voice again.

"No!" said Clive scornfully.

"You're not ok?" asked Charlotte.

"No, I am ok. It's fine just a bit of a headache that's all," responded Clive.

"So what are you going to do about him then?" asked Charlotte again.

"I don't know. I guess if the police aren't able to dish out the justice then I'll have to do it myself," he said.

The man was trying to say something that was muffled through the tape. Charlotte slapped him across his face.

"Thank you Injustice Cure. My hero," she said as she leant her back against him pushing her rear into his crotch as her hands grabbed his arms and pulled them round her waist. "You're my protector Injustice Cure and I owe you my life. You can have anything I can give you and I mean anything," she said letting out a breathy sigh as she finished her sentence.

"Kill the man. He is no good to this world," said the voice in Clive's head. The combination of the voice's commands and Charlotte's persuasive methods was hard to resist.

Clive picked up a butcher's knife from the counter underneath the diet sheet for the tiger and grasped it tightly in his right hand. His vision was out of focus and he walked forward feeling like a passenger in his own actions.

"You're not supposed to put the tape over my nose as well. I couldn't bloody well breathe," shouted the man who had sweated away the adhesiveness of the tape. "Oh you have a knife that's right I'm supposed to be pleading for my life now. Help! Help!" he added but there was no distress evident on his face.

The strange, unconcerned attitude of the man puzzled Clive and suddenly his mind cleared like he had just woken from a dream. He looked at the red face of the man in the chair who was panting for breath. Clive dropped the knife on to the counter. "I can't do it," he said.

"You disappoint me Clive," said the voice inside Clive's head except it wasn't inside his head. It was behind him.

Clive turned to face Charlotte but instead he saw a huge, strong black man with furious eyes staring at him. His teeth were clenched and his chest pumping with heavy breathing. It was the same guy from the hospital and now Clive remembered where he had recognised him from before then. He was the zoo keeper who gave Clive the injection after the attack.

"Where's Charlotte?" asked Clive.

"I asked you to do this one thing for me, the man who created you. I saved your life and this is how you repay me," said the man.

"Who are you? I think you've got the wrong guy," said Clive his voice shrinking as fast as his bravery.

"Who am I?" said the man pointing to himself and cocking his head to one side. "I am your creator. This is the man who you see before you."

Clive grabbed the knife, turned and ran towards the open door of the refrigerator pulling it shut behind him as he jumped inside. His fear of being shut inside a fridge was insignificant compared to his fear of that man. He stood with his back against the wall facing the door, the knife held out in front of him ready to defend himself if the scary man came for him.

Chapter 14

Clive checked his watch. It had been twenty minutes since he shut himself inside the refrigerator and his fingers were starting to go numb with the cold. He looked around at the bits of vegetables, defrosting meat and jars of liquids on the metal shelving inside the refrigerator hoping to keep his mind off the cold but it was no use. He had to get out. Luckily for him the manufacturers had envisioned his nightmare scenario of being locked in and there was a handle on the inside.

He cautiously opened the door and stuck his head out.

"It's ok he's gone. You can come out now," said the man still tied to the chair.

"Are you sure?" Clive asked.

"Jeez. So much of a superhero you are. Runs away from trouble," mocked the man. "Now untie me."

"Wait. Who are you?" asked Clive stopping in his tracks.

"Untie me and I'll explain. I think you cut the circulation to my hands off when you tied these things."

"How do I know I can trust you?" asked Clive.

"Seriously? After all that and you still think I'm the bad guy?"

Clive used the knife to slice through the cable ties holding the man's wrists together. The man pumped his hands to get the blood flowing again and rubbed the thick red indents on his wrists.

"Talk," said Clive pointing the knife at the man.

"Before I do, out of curiosity, why did you call me a sick pervert? Is it the beard?" asked the man.

"No it's because you'd been stalking Charlotte."

"Ah. The old damsel in distress angle," said the man shaking his head.

"Who are you?" asked Clive again.

"My name is Robinson Henley-Wilde. Pleased to meet you," Robinson held out his hand for Clive to shake it but Clive didn't respond.

"Who was that guy?"

"That guy? I don't but that girl was Charlotte Temple. I used to work with her father in our pharmaceutical laboratory," said Robinson.

"Why are you stalking her?" asked Clive still waving the knife at the man.

"I'm not stalking her. I'm trying to help her."

"Help her with what?"

"How long have you known Charlotte for?" asked Robinson.

"Not long. I saved her from being mugged," answered Clive proudly.

"Well, Charlotte's father and I were worked together for 30 years so I've known her since she was born."

"That still doesn't explain what you're trying to help her with."

"I'm getting to that. Me and her father were working on a new drug that would treat mental illness. Her father claimed to have made an important discovery, one that would revolutionise the treatment of mental illness but he became secretive and withdrawn, wouldn't share any of his research with me or anyone else except Charlotte. She'd been visiting the lab more frequently than usual until his recent death."

"How did he die?"

"He died in a caving accident which was strange because I never knew he was a caver."

"What has this got to do with Charlotte?" asked Clive.

"Charlotte is a schizophrenic!"

"What! No way," said Clive lowering the knife to his side.

"Yeah way. You don't know her much, do you?" asked the man, giving Clive a concerned father look.

"So you want to send her to an asylum?" asked Clive raising the knife at his captor again.

"I think her father tested the new drug directly on her. I need to get her to the lab so I can analyse her blood. If she has been given this new drug then she could be in danger. It hasn't undergone any testing and could be doing anything to her body."

"Could she die?" asked Clive.

"Possibly. If not in the short term then maybe it's done lasting damage in the long term. I need to find her and get her to my lab. Her father was a good friend of mine. I owe it to him to keep her safe."

"Then I'll help you," said Clive.

"Do you want to put down the knife first?"

Clive placed the knife back on the counter. "Sorry," he said. "Can I ask you a question?"

"Sure," said Robinson.

"You said you need to analyse her blood. Could you tell if there was something wrong with anyone's blood?"

"I'm a scientist. Of course I can!" answered Robinson.

Chapter 15

Robinson put the slide under his microscope and slowly adjusted the knobs on the side. Unable to share Robinson's view, Clive looked around the lab to occupy himself. He was disappointed that there were no steaming beakers of green liquid sat over Bunsen burners and connected to a complicated web of tubes and glassware. Instead it was all grey and white, clean with lots of small machines and computers which gave nothing away about their purpose.

"Interesting," Robinson said.

"What?" asked Clive still holding the piece of cotton wool to his arm where the blood had been drawn.

"You have traces of an accelerant in your blood."

"What does that mean?"

"It's a type of chemical that works with another chemical reaction to speed it up."

"And that's interesting why?"

"That's interesting because accelerants are used in chemistry to assist with producing mass amounts of drugs. They're a commercial product designed to work in very specific reactions. No one's ever documented them working in a human being before, not to this extent anyway. It seems to have completely fused within your blood. Remarkable."

"What does all this mean?" asked Clive as he perched one of his buttocks on the tiny stool next to the counter top.

"It means that certain chemical reactions within your body take place 100's of times faster than they would in a normal human being. Tell me you've noticed something strange about your body?"

Clive lifted up the cotton wool and showed his arm to Robinson. "Is the fact I have no puncture wound where you stuck the needle in strange?"

Robinson examined his arm carefully. "That would tie in with my theory. Your cell production could be working at an increased rate."

"That's nothing," said Clive picking up a scalpel, "watch this." Clive slowly dragged the scalpel across his finger. A straight red line of blood appeared on his finger. He stuck his finger in his mouth and sucked the blood away before presenting it to Robinson.

"It's healed," said Robinson stepping back in astonishment.

Clive smiled in delight at the effect of his party trick.

"Have you always been able to do this?" asked Robinson.

"No. It's only since I was attacked by a hyena. "

"A hyena?" asked Robinson confused.

"It was at the zoo. Long story," said Clive. "The doctor's said I recovered faster than anyone they've ever seen."

Robinson grabbed his face in one hand and rubbed his beard. "I'm not aware of any particularly complex chemicals within a hyena. Just your standard mammal, but I could be wrong," said Robinson as he turned to his computer to look it up.

"I don't think it was the hyena. I think it was what happened after the attack," said Clive.

Robinson spun his chair back round to face Clive. "You think it was a drug given to you at the hospital?"

"Not at the hospital, at the zoo."

"Why would you be taking drugs at the zoo? You're not a user are you?" asked Robinson disappointingly.

"No I'm not a user," answered Clive with a degree of offence in his voice. "You know the black guy we saw earlier?"

"Yes."

"I think he injected me with something after the attack and I think I saw him in the hospital whilst I was recovering. I wasn't sure before because I thought I was hallucinating but after seeing him tonight I know it definitely happened."

"Then we need to find him and find out what he's injected you with exactly. I don't want to scare you but there are a number of chemical reactions in the body that, if sped up at the rate yours are sped up, could kill you."

Clive feels dizzy and he thinks about how insignificant his superhero aspirations are now. He'd started the night thinking about a new life with a new woman, then that was taken away with the news he might be a father and now he could die before the baby is born. *One in one out*, thought Clive, seems fair but at the same time it's not fair. It's not fair at all.

Chapter 16

The morning was breaking as Clive left Robinson's lab and he had to dodge the rush hour as he made his way back to his house. Clive figured Lila would probably be sat up waiting for him to come home.

"Lila. I'm back," shouted Clive as he dropped his balaclava on the table and flopped on to the couch.

He switched on the news half expecting to see something about his encounter at the zoo but instead it was a piece on global warming so Clive switched it over to a music channel.

"Lila," he shouted but there was no response.

He got off the couch and went to the bottom of the stairs. "Lila," he shouted again and paused for a response, silence. He ran upstairs and looked in all the rooms. Her phone was on the bed but she wasn't anywhere to be seen. He rushed back down the stairs and into the kitchen. On the side was a note:

'Bring Robinson to 328 Broadstone Way. I have Lila.'

Chapter 17

Clive see's the shiny bald head and straggly beard of Robinson leaving his lab and slams the brakes on.

"Get in," he shouts at Robinson.

"It'll be 20 bucks to party with me sailor," says Robinson sarcastically.

"Shut up and get in," shouts Clive in his angry superhero voice.

Robinson jumps in the car and Clive floors it, spinning the wheels on his little Hyundai.

"We're going after the black guy," said Clive.

"So soon. Let's find Charlotte first then the black guy."

"He's kidnapped my wife," said Clive through gritted teeth.

"Oh!"

They reached the address on the note in silence and Clive yanked the handbrake on before they'd stopped, locking the back wheels and drawing a long, black number 11 in the road. The building was an old grey abandoned square industrial building with a tall tower in the middle. The last person to use this building had left a long time ago and bricked up all the windows before they left. The front door was less secure and dangled crookedly from one hinge.

"Come on. Let's go," Clive urged to Robinson as he got out the car.

"I'm moving as fast as I can. I'm a scientist you know we aren't renowned for our physical prowess and speed."

Clive burst through the front door creating a wave of dust as it dropped from its last hinge and slammed on the floor.

"I am in here," said the Nigerian voice from down the corridor.

Clive grabbed Robinson by the scruff of his leather jacket and dragged him down the corridor hurdling over debris as he went. The end of the corridor opened out into a large hall with shafts of bright light breaking through the cracks in the ceiling and illuminating dust clouds which spiralled up into the air.

Clive shoved Robinson out into the open.

"What's this?" Robinson asked.

"I'm sorry," he answered, "he's got my wife."

"Clive," shouted Lila.

Clive looked up to see his wife suspended 30 feet in the air inside a metal cage that served as an elevator to the top of the tower.

"You let her down now," shouted Clive.

"Mr Silver. There is no need for your voice to be raised. I will decide what happens now."

Clive's eyes started to well up. He remembered the worries Lila had about him becoming a superhero, the concerns she had for his safety. He'd shrugged it all off thinking his super healing would mean he'd come to no real harm but he'd never considered the danger he might be putting Lila at, and the baby.

"Who are you?" asked Clive.

"I am Jago, but that is not important."

"Look Jago, you've got what you wanted now let her go," he urged. The usual menace in his superhero voice was softened by the trembling of his lip.

"Mr Silver I would not hurt a hair on her head. She is safe, but I need your cooperation." Jago throws a pair of handcuffs to Clive. "Put these on him."

Clive snapped one link round Robinson's wrist. "Don't worry sweetheart. It's going to be ok," he called to Lila as he put the second link on Robinsons other wrist. "Right done. Now let her down."

Jago pressed a button on a remote and a mechanical motor whirred into action lowering the cage slowly.

"Unfortunately Mr Silver I'm going to have to make sure that you don't get in the way of my plans either."

Two arms wrapped themselves around him from behind. Clive felt his arms being pinned to his side and his whole body squeezed like a tube of toothpaste. Clive looked down and saw the huge digger arm sized limbs with thin silvery skin stretched over each of the many mountains of muscle spread along their length.

"Meet my friend Mr Rick Stones," said Jago. "He now does the job that I created you to do Clive."

Robinson looked the man up and down "Let me guess, bodybuilder on steroids?" he asked.

"Want me to smash your face in, ass-wipe," growled Rick in a deep noise that sounded as though his throat was lined with rubble.

Jago laughed. "Easy my friend. We do not need to kill these men to accomplish our goals. We are non violent."

Rick snorted like a frustrated bull and squeezed Clive tighter. Clive heard a cracking noise and felt a pain stab into his lower back.

The cage had now lowered to the ground and Rick threw Clive into it followed by Robinson before shutting the door.

"Now there is no one to get in my way," said Jago with menace.

"Jago wait. What are you going to do? It doesn't need to be like this you know," said Robinson pressing his face between the bars of the cage.

"You were a good friend to my father I'm sorry it has to be like this," said Jago and he pressed the button on the lift controls to raise the cage again.

Robinson's face screwed up in confusion as he tried to remember if he knew anyone with a son named Jago.

The cage started to ascend and Clive looked down at the slowly shrinking Rick Stones. He was like an exaggerated action figure of a wrestler with skin stretched so thing the veins and arteries were visible beneath. His face looked angry and he was almost boiling with rage.

"What's his problem?" said Clive quietly.

"It's the accelerated chemical reaction. Steroids grows muscles but in certain circumstances it also causes rage as well as, ahem, other side effects," Robinson punctuated his sentence with a raise of the eyebrows.

"Eek," said Clive with a smile as he waved his little finger in the air whilst below him Jago and Rick left the building.

He remembered Lila was in the cage with them, untied her and hugged her closely to his chest.

When he let go she beat her fist against him. "You asshole I told you no good would come of this superhero nonsense. We've tried for so long for this baby and now we're pregnant and I'm stuck in a cage hanging from a ceiling and it's stressing me out. You're supposed to be looking after me not putting me at risk."

"You say you've been trying for a baby and now you're pregnant, interesting. Did you have a sperm count done before the hyena incident?" asked Robinson.

"Not now," snapped Clive.

"Who is this?" asked Lila.

"He's a scientist," answers Clive.

"Robinson Henley-Wilde, pleased to meet you," says Robinson extending his hand out to Lila.

Lila looks at the crumbs in his tangled beard and his dirty, cracked leather jacket. She decides against touching him. "Get us out of here Clive," she says.

"How?" he asked.

"I don't know. Use your superpowers or something," she said holding her forehead with stress.

"I don't have the power to fly."

"It's just like the Hyena enclosure again. You're such a coward, I wish Brian were here he'd save me," she said. "I bet if Charlotte rang you right now you'd find a way out to get to her."

Robinson chuckled.

"What's he laughing at?" said Lila angrily.

"I don't know," answered Clive. Lila had wound him up. He was ten times the hero Brian was. "I've got an idea. Stand back," he said and pushed Lila and Robinson back. He opened the cage door, grabbed hold of the sides of the opening, closed his eyes and took a breath.

"I hope you're not going to do what I think you're going to do," said Lila.

Clive jumped and fell through the air, landing suddenly with two loud snaps that echoed through the empty building as he hit the floor from 30 feet up.

"Argh!" he screamed at the top of his voice. Somewhere, in the girders holding up the roof, a bird flapped off its perch.

"Clive are you alright?" shouted Lila from the cage above him.

"Do I look alright?" he shouted back. He tried to stand up but as soon as he put any weight on his leg it folded over and he fell back to the floor. He looked down at his legs and noticed that his toes were almost touching his thighs and his shins were bent in half. He straightened his legs out, wincing and groaning as he did so before his head felt like it was floating above his shoulders and he passed out.

"Clive, Clive," shouted Robinson.

Clive opened his eyes and rubbed his face. His head hurt but the feeling was fading fast. He looked up in the air above him and noticed the cage remembering where he was. He jumped to his feet only realising then that his legs had healed. He pressed the button on the elevator control and it descended to the floor.

Lila jumped out of the cage and hugged him. "Thank you," she said and she kissed him on the lips.

"Yeah thank you," said Robinson.

"No need for you to kiss me," said Clive to Robinson.

"OK enough of this fluffy stuff, we need to stop Jago," said Robinson.

"Oh no. Me and Clive are going home," said Lila linking arms with her husband.

"But I can't do this on my own," said Robinson, his eyes looking worried.

"He's right baby. I need to stop this guy before he hurts someone. I want my baby to grow up in a city where people care for each other. I'd be hypocritical if I wished for that and didn't do the same myself."

"But how are you going to beat his friend, the he-man? He's huge and did you see how strong he was? He damn near broke your back without breaking a sweat."

"I don't know but I've got to try."

"I'm not happy about this," she said. "But you've gotta do what you've gotta do," she added with a soft smile at him.

"Thanks baby," he said back grabbing her hands.

"Can I stop you before you break out into song or something because this is getting sickly. We need to stop Jago fast before he does something bad," said Robinson.

"Right. Do you have any ideas where he'll be?" asked Clive.

"I think I got an idea. Let's go."

Chapter 18

"So which way?" asked Clive as he jumped back in the car and fired up his Hyundai.

"Head up to the mountains," responded Robinson, "I think the chemical Jago injected you with has something to do with what Charlotte's father was working on."

Clive slammed his foot to the floor. The little car jumped forward slightly but then wheezed as it ran out of the power needed to continue its acceleration.

"If you're going to be fighting crime more often I'd recommend a faster car," said Robinson.

Clive shot an unhappy look at Robinson.

"Just saying, that's all," Robinson said in his defence.

Ahead of them a truck was driving down the middle of the road towards them.

"Hey! What's this guy's problem," Clive said as he flashed his lights and honked his horn.

The truck didn't move over, instead it got closer and closer getting larger and larger. Robinson grabbed the sides of his seat and braced his feet against the dash. They were about to collide when Clive swerved. His car rumbled as two of the tyres rode in the dirt at the side of the road before the truck passed and he pulled it back on to the road.

Robinson and Clive looked behind them to see the large tanker disappearing down the road behind them.

"Jeez, some guys think they own the road. As if this isn't hard enough already!" said Clive.

Robinson directed them to the entrance of the cave where Charlotte's father had been killed. Police tape was still tied to the fence by the entrance.

Clive grabbed his torch from the pockets of his trousers and ran in to the cave followed by Robinson.

"That way," said Robinson pointing down a passageway to the right.

They soon found themselves stumbling over rocks and rubble as they made their way down the passage until it opened out into a cave of orange rock. The bottom of the cave was smooth and sunk into a depression like an empty swimming pool.

Robinson grabbed Clive's hand and directed his torch down the jagged wall of the cave. Halfway down the depression was a line where the jagged wall met smooth wall which was darker than the top half of the cave.

"This has been recently drained," said Robinson.

"What does that mean?" said Clive in disbelief.

"It's been drained, as in the water has been taken out of it."

"I know what drained means. What does it mean for our situation?"

"Oh. Well things are worse, a lot worse. Whatever Jago's planning its big if he's needs this much accelerant," said Robinson.

"Accelerant!" exclaimed Clive. "This was a pool of accelerant?"

"I think so and I think that's what Charlotte's father had stumbled upon and this was what he was coming back for when he was killed."

"OK we need to find Jago. Where else would he be?"

"I don't know!" answered Robinson.

"Think. You have to think. The city is in danger," exclaimed Clive grabbing Robinson by the shoulders and shaking him.

"Well he'd need some method of transporting and storing this amount of liquid so I guess that's a place to start," said Robinson starting a train of thought.

"The tanker," interrupted Clive.

Robinson's face turned serious as he understood Clive's idea.

"Let's go," said Robinson.

Chapter 19

They reached the section of road where they'd nearly been run off by the tanker.

"What now?" asked Clive.

"If the tanker was heading in this direction then whatever he's planning to do must also be in this direction," answered Robinson stating the obvious, "What's down this road? Think industrial sites maybe, laboratories, anywhere that might hold a large quantity of liquid."

"What like the water plant?" asked Clive.

"Of course! Why didn't I think of that?" said Robinson as he slapped his hand on his forehead, "Let's go!"

They reached the water plant. The gates were closed, the metal bent and twisted together to lock them in place.

"That's Jago's goon's work," said Robinson, "You're going to have to ram them."

"What? No way. This car's only 6 month's old. I've still got payments to make on it," complained Clive.

"If Jago empties the contents of that tanker into the water supply then can you imagine the consequences? Every person on medication will mutate into a super being or worse it could kill them. It's not worth thinking about."

Clive closed his eyes, bit his bottom lip and let out a sigh. He reversed the car back 50 metres and slipped the car into drive. He revved the engine a couple of times, dropped the handbrake and floored it towards the gates.

The acceleration of the small, economical run-around was the opposite of the lightning fast battering ram that they needed and as they approached the gates Clive doubted that they were even going fast enough to make it through.

The car hit the blue iron gates with a crash, shooting the car sideways as the momentum was redirected by the immovable gates. The airbags popped and Clive and Robinson face planted into them before bouncing back against their seats.

"Well that didn't work," said Clive looking at Robinson.

"I'll say it again. You need a faster car."

They two men got out and approached the gate.

"We're going to have to climb it," said Clive.

"Do I look like a man that can climb things," answered Robinson.

Clive grabs Robinson's legs and hoisted him up quickly before he could complain, throwing him up to the top of the gate. Robinson hooked his arms over the top of the gate and rested his weight on his armpits. Clive jumped up and pulled himself over the gate so he was sat on top of it. He pulled Robinson over and lowered him down the over side before jumping down himself.

"We should have done this the first time before we totalled my car," said Clive.

They slowly crept round the side of a guard hut and Robinson peered through the window. The old security guard was tied against a table leg inside.

"Yeah Jago's here, alright," said Robinson.

They carried on into the plant and found the tanker parked next to a large square pool of water.

"That's where the water is held before it's sent through the filters, into the water supply of the city," said Robinson. "We need to find out if Jago's added the accelerant yet."

"Now then ladies. Have you come to play?" said a voice behind Clive and Robinson.

They turned to see Rick Stones stood facing them. His shirtless torso was as wide as it was tall with muscles twitching in waves across his body. His eyes were manic, staring like a man on the ultimate sugar rush. His clenched fists were the size of basketballs. He stepped slowly toward them.

"I don't know what you've got in this Rick, but let's all calm down and talk about this," said Clive calmly.

"Talk? Talk? You sound like my probation officer, you little weed," growled Rick as the pressure built up inside him and he exploded with a punch aimed at the side of the tanker splitting its side. The tanker was empty.

"Well now we know the water's tainted," whispered Robinson through the side of this mouth.

"You should've stayed in that cage where you were safe," said Rick. His face had calmed slightly from before but as he took each step forward the anger grew.

Clive ran and hid behind some water tanks wrapped in steel cages followed by Robinson.

"What are you doing?" asked Robinson.

"I can't beat this guy look at me, I'm half the size of one of his legs. This is time for flight not fight," he said. The old Clive Silver was back, running away from his fears.

"But we can't stop now we need to find Jago and prevent him finishing what he's started," pleaded Robinson. "What happened to The Injustice Cure? Is he only the brave hero when there's a pretty lady around?"

Clive's phone rang in his pocket, it was Lila. He grabbed it and quickly switched it to silent.

"There you are," said Rick as he threw the water tank aside exposing Clive and Robinson's hiding place.

"Run," said Clive but it was too late. Rick grabbed him by the leg and swung him round his head like cowboy's lasso before letting go, shooting Clive into the concrete wall of a building.

Clive tenderly got to his feet and started running away from the goliath who, thankfully, wasn't as fast as he was strong.

Rick kept swinging his fists at Clive but Clive managed to duck or swerve each one and would skip away to the next bit of cover or hiding place he could go, making frightened whimpering noises as he fled.

Clive hid behind some crates and listened for the crashing footsteps of Rick. They were stomping around but not in any particular direction. He was safe here for a while.

"Where are you, pipsqueak?" Rick shouted.

Clive's hands were trembling. He felt his phone vibrate in his pocket. The feeling made him jump. It was a message, 'I'm sorry for being so negative about what you're trying to do. Whatever you want to do I'll always support you. I do love you and I want you to know that you're already my hero x x x Lila and bump ;-)'. The hairs on the back of his neck stood up and he felt his tear ducts swell as they tried to push out a tear. Clive struggled with his fear. He had always struggled with his fear and had always opted for the safe way out. A father needs to protect his child at all costs. It's his basic instinct. Clive couldn't take the coward's way out for ever. Now was the time to prove himself.

Clive walked round the crate and stood out in the open.

"I'm ready for you fatso," said Clive.

"Fatso? Fatso? This is pure lean muscle," growled Rick as he tensed his whole body up and let out a roar. The roar went on and grew to a deep rumble like a truck engine. Clive was surprised at the power of the roar until he realised that it was actually a truck engine and it was reversing at speed towards Rick. He was too slow to get out of the way and truck hit him carrying him backwards until it hit the wall of the big concrete building, crushing Rick between the two giant objects.

Robinson jumped out of the truck. "You're welcome," he said.

Clive ran round to the back of the mangled truck. "Is he dead?" asked Clive.

"I don't know but let's not hang around to find out. Let's go get Jago."

"We need to split up," said Clive. He'd always heard people say this in films and it had always seemed like a bad idea to him, safety in numbers is always better but right now it meant they could cover ground faster.

"I'll go this way," said Robinson and ran into the concrete building.

A mechanical noise started and the water in the pool started bubbling. Clive ran up the metal stairs that led to the platform overlooking the pools.

"Clive," said a voice from the top of the platform. It was Charlotte.

Clive picked up his pace and reached the platform at the top of the tower to see Jago leaning over the side looking down into the white water below.

"What have you done with Charlotte?" asked Clive knowing that there was no way off the platform other than the way he came.

Clive looked into the swirling white water below hoping to see Charlotte swimming to safety.

"Charlotte," he called over the side.

Jago laughed a deep, hearty laugh.

Clive had to stop him but he had to save Charlotte. He knew if he didn't fight Jago now then he'd always be a coward. This was the time to prove himself. He hoped Charlotte would be safe and prayed for Robinson to come back and rescue her.

Clive lunged at Jago but Jago ducked out of the way leaving Clive to slam on to the control panel. Jago pulled a hand held switch out of his pocket and smiled at Clive. He flicked the switch and the control panel exploded beneath Clive throwing him over the barrier of the platform and into the water below.

Clive hit the water and felt his body being pulled under the swirling torrent. His head pounded from the blast of the control panel. He remembered Charlotte had fallen in here and knew he must find her. He pulled himself to the surface and took a deep breath before going under again. He opened his eyes but the movement in the water meant that he couldn't see a thing. He came up for breath again and looked around on the surface, hoping for a clue where Charlotte might be.

"Clive, Clive," shouted Robinson from the edge.

"I've got to save Charlotte," he shouted back. His tears were mixing with the water on his soaking balaclava.

"No you need shut off the pump. The accelerant is in the water supply."

"I need to save Charlotte first," said Clive diving below the surface again.

Clive swam all the way to the bottom of the tank and felt himself being pulled strongly into one corner. The current was being created by the spinning propeller of a pump draining the water away. Next to it he saw a ladder that was used to get to the pump when the water was drained. Clive grabbed the ladder and pulled himself up against the current and to the top.

"Shut off the pump," shouted Robinson. "You need to save the city."

Clive tears streamed faster and his eyes struggled to see clearly. He knew he had to shut off the pump before it contaminated an entire city but to do that he had to give up on Charlotte. Was the life of a woman he loved worth more than the lives of an entire city? He realised then that he'd admitted to himself that he loved Charlotte.

Robinson ran up the stairs to the metal platform where Jago was stood blocking his way.

"Move out of my way. Your father wouldn't have wanted this," said Robinson.

Jago smiled and stood to the side letting Robinson through. He went to the control panel to shut off the pump and saw that it was destroyed.

"Why? Why did you do this?" Robinson asked.

"If everyone is like me then I won't be different anymore and people won't call me crazy," Jago replied.

"This isn't the way."

A muffled grinding noise followed by a loud bang came from below the platform. The water settled down in its tank.

Jago and Robinson ran down the stairs to see Clive emerge from the water tank. Behind him the water was red. Clive's right arm was a bloodied mangle of flesh, and bone was visible through the deep lacerations.

"I blocked the pump," said Clive as his chest heaved and his eyes burned with rage. "I think that shorted the motor. Can't find Charlotte though. She must've been sucked through the pump and, well, look what it did to my arm," he held up his arm which was already looking in better shape than before.

"Look Clive you need to calm down," said Robinson walking towards him.

"He killed her!" shouted Clive pointing in Jago's direction with his undamaged hand.

"Clive you need to calm down. We can deal with this," pleaded Robinson.

"Damn right we need to deal with this," said Clive. He had no thoughts of being afraid. No fears of being in a fight. He had nothing he valued more right now than avenging Charlotte. This, he decided, was what it felt like to be brave. He pulled his pen knife from his pocket and ran at Jago stabbing the blade straight into his heart.

Jago dropped to the ground clutching the knife stuck in his chest. Clive turned and started walking away.

"What have you done?" screamed Robinson running over to Jago.

Clive realised something wasn't right. There was more concern in Robinson's voice than he expected, too much sympathy for the guy who was planning to destroy a city. He turned to see Charlotte lying on the floor where Jago had fallen. The knife was stuck in her chest and she was bleeding out fast.

Clive dropped to his knees and threw up a big mouthful of water. "How?" he said.

"The accelerant. In your case it mutated your healing, in hers it mutated the schizophrenia. Jago was her alternative personality."

"Why didn't you say?" cried Clive.

"I was trying to and you just jumped in."

"We need to save her," said Clive. He reached into his pockets and pulled out the bandages and held them out in his trembling hands for Robinson to take.

"These aren't enough to save her and I'm a scientist not a doctor," said Robinson solemnly.

"Then we need to get her to a hospital." Clive picked her up. Her arms and legs flopped either side of his arms.

Robinson put his hand on Clive's shoulder to stop him. "No. There's nothing they can do for her but we might be able to save her. I've got an idea but it's a long shot."

"You've got try it."

Chapter 20

Robinson cleared a space on the bench in his lab, sweeping the existing contents on to the floor. Clive laid Charlotte's body down on it. Already she had begun to go cold and her lips turned blue as her body went into shock.

Robinson ran off and came back clutching a handful of tubes and syringes.

"Give me your arm," Robinson said to Clive. He tied a tourniquet around Clive's arm and jabbed a needle in hard and deep, venting some of his frustration at Clive for causing all this. The blood ran out of Clive's arm down the tube and stopped at a closed valve in the tube.

Robinson delicately put a needle into Charlottes arm and connected the tube from Clive.

"Stand up. You need to be higher than her," said Robinson.

Clive pulled over a chair and stood on it. Robinson opened the tap and the blood raced down the tube and into Lila's body.

"Will this save her?" asked Clive.

"I hope so but there's a good chance her body will reject your blood."

"What about the knife?" asked Clive.

Robinson looked closely at the knife sticking out of Lila's chest. "You still got those bandages?"

Clive pulled them out of his pocket and handed them to Robinson who folded them over and over making a thick pad.

Robinson put his hands around the knife and looked up at Clive. "Let's hope this blood of yours is good stuff," he said and he slowly withdrew the knife before quickly pressing the pad of bandages down on the wound. The pad slowly turned red as it soaked up the blood.

They both stood and watched the motionless body of Charlotte. "How will we know it's worked?" asked Clive.

"When she doesn't die," said Robinson.

Clive felt butterflies in his stomach and a metallic taste in his mouth. "How much longer do I need to do this?" he asked Robinson.

"This isn't something I've done before so I'd say as long as possible," he answered.

"Ok," said Clive closing his eyes and concentrating on not passing out. He opened them again quickly as he felt himself falling to one side.

"You doing ok?" asked Robinson.

"I'm fine. How is she?"

Robinson put his fingers on her neck feeling for a pulse. He shook his head.

"We need to keep trying," said Clive.

Clive's head spun. He felt as though it'd been spinning for hours and he wanted nothing more than for it to stop. He swayed around on the chair before tumbling to the ground hard and unconscious.

Chapter 21

Clive woke up on the floor of Robinson's lab. His head was laid on a folded up lab coat. He sat up quickly then took a moment for the rush of blood to his head to subside.

"What happened?" he asked.

"You passed out there. Probably took a bit too much blood from you," answered Robinson.

"Charlotte," said Clive as he jumped to his feet and looked on the counter. Her face had regained its colour and her lips had gone back to the beautiful crimson red that they had been before.

"She's doing well," said Robinson as he stood beside Clive. "Her pulse is normal and look at this." Robinson pulled her shirt aside exposing a scar across her heart.

"It's healed. It worked," said Clive excitedly as he hugged Robinson.

"Whoa slow down there," said Robinson uncomfortable with the human contact.

"So what happens now?" asked Clive.

"I'll keep her here. Keep an eye on her until she wakes up," said Robinson.

"And then?"

"And then I try to rebuild her life. Get her back on her normal treatment and hope she stabilises. In the meantime I need to analyse her blood, make sure that this accelerant hasn't done any lasting damage. Same goes for you. I have a sample of your blood already so I'll be in touch when I know more about what's happening to you. In the meantime go home, get some rest and keep out of trouble."

"OK. Keep in touch. I'll come back and visit her," said Clive. A wave of happiness washed over him.

"I don't think that's wise," said Robinson.

Clive's wave crashed. "Why not?" he asked.

"Charlotte will have enough to deal with in the coming months without complicating things by getting involved with a married man. A married man with a baby on the way I might add," said Robinson looking into Clive's eyes. The protective father look was chiselled on Robinson's face.

"What are you talking about? We're just friends," said Clive as he broke eye contact with Robinson and looked at his feet.

"Go home Clive," said Robinson. "Go back to your pregnant wife. Charlotte will be a different person in a few weeks. Different to the girl you saved. You're best forgetting about her."

Clive touched Robinsons arm. He knew his new friend was right. "Thanks for saving her," he said as he turned to leave.

"Oh and Clive," called Robinson.

"Yeah?"

"That was quite a brave thing you know. holding out during that blood transfusion. She took 4 pints from you, most people would have passed out a lot sooner than you did or even died from losing that much blood. Real brave stuff."

Clive smiled and left the lab.

Chapter 22

Clive walked in the house and had déjà vu of the last time he came in when Lila had been kidnapped.

"Lila," he called. There was silence. "Lila," he shouted again this time with more panic.

"I'm up here," said the familiar voice of Lila.

Clive ran up the stairs and found her in the bathroom. She hugged him tightly. "Thank god you're safe," she said as her eyes examined him for damage. "Look," she held up a strange white stick that looked a little like a toothbrush but without the bristles.

"What is it?" he asked.

"It's a pregnancy test," she stood beside him, put her head next to his and pointed at a little window in the stick. "You see that line? That means I'm pregnant!" she said jumping up and down at the end of her sentence.

Clive smiled, hugged her and then kissed her.

"Does it say if it's a boy or a girl?" he asked.

"No silly. It's just a few cells at the moment. It'll be weeks before it becomes a he or a she."

Clive felt a wash of tiredness come over his body. He needed sleep.

"You look shattered." Lila said.

"Yeah I'm a little tired," he said and kissed her on the head.

"I'd run you a bath but I'm pregnant now so I need to put my feet up. Plus I gotta call my mom and tell her the good news," said Lila and followed it up with a little squeal of delight.

Lila left the room. Clive looked in the mirror and saw the huge bags under his eyes. He yawned and sat down on the floor of the bathroom.

He'd proved to himself that he can be brave. He'd put himself in danger, he'd fought with criminals, been shot, crashed his car, lost half his blood. He'd nearly lost it all tonight, Lila, Charlotte, the baby even his own life and maybe the entire city. He didn't give up though and he fought to save them. He chose to act, do the right thing, be a good citizen and a good husband. That was brave.

The End

About

If you enjoyed this book please leave a review so that more people may be persuaded to enjoy it too. If you'd like to know more about the author, Luke George, you can follow his blog:

www.boredism.co.uk